The Muddy
Waters
Of Vietnam

BY

Marshall Huffman

The Muddy Waters of Vietnam©2017
by MW Huffman

All rights reserved

The Muddy Waters of Vietnam

OTHER BOOKS BY MW HUFFMAN

Angie Bartoni Case File #15 - RAGE
Angie Bartoni Case File #16 - The Inheritance
Angie Bartoni Case File #17 - Abduction
Angie Bartoni Case File #18 - Imminent Attack
Angie Bartoni Case File #19 - Campground Killer
Angie Bartoni Case File #20 - Subterfuge
Angie Bartoni Case File #21 - Human Cargo
Angie Bartoni Case File #22 - Attack on America
Angie Bartoni Case File #23 - Dead Drop
The Logan Files - Blond Deception
The Logan Files - Innocence and Avarice
The Logan Files - The Deal Breaker
The Logan Files - Pain Center
The Logan Files - The Rose Tattoo
Norris Files - Insurrection
Norris Files - Silver2
WHEN EVIL KNOCKS
Broken Justice
A-121 VIRUS
Race for the Bomb

THE MUDDY WATERS
OF VIETNAM

PROLOGUE

Unlike WWII, Americans were not behind the soldiers, airmen, and sailors that fought in Korea and Vietnam. Not only were they treated with contempt by a large portion of the population, they were shunned when they returned. These military men and women had not 'won' the war so they were considered unworthy of any accolades.

This story is dedicated to the Vietnam era veterans. It is a work of fiction based upon research and is not meant to depict any one PBR river patrol boat. This is a fictional story of the Brown Water Naval Forces.

The author hopes it is received in the spirt it was intended, to shed a little light on what transpired along the Mekong Delta. The author served in the Navy from 1964 – 1972.

*Author's Note: The 'F' word has been omitted from this book. As a former Navy MM1 I know it is used almost non-stop. I find it offers little to the main story line.

CHAPTER ONE

Standing on the observation deck of the Aircraft Carrier USS Ticonderoga (CVA-14) was a favorite pastime for a lot of sailors not associated with the flight deck operations. We would go up and watch as the planes landed and jerk to a stop by the arresting cables. Equally impressive was the launch of the aircraft. Zero to airborne in less than three seconds.

The Ticonderoga was more than a ship. It was actually a floating city. It had a crew of roughly 3,200 sailors for normal operation and the 7th Air Wing, comprised of another 2,100 men. Add in 70 or so Flag and Staff Officers, and a further 70 Marines, and it's easy to understand how massive the ship is.

As a Machinist Mate First Class, I spent most of my time in the engine rooms. I stood watch over the overall operation and kept an eye on the throttle men. Manning the throttles can be tricky when launching aircraft. Generally, we are running at full or flank speed, which for our ship, was in excess of 30 knots an hour. When the planes launched, the steam pressure would drop and it was one of the jobs of the throttle man to keep a close eye on the pressure. If the pressure fell too low, it could suck a boiler offline and that would cripple the ship. Obviously, the Captain would seriously frown on such an occurrence.

I had taken the Chief's test and was anxiously waiting to find out the results. Just passing the test did not guarantee you would get the promotion. It depended on a whole list of criteria. Things such as your fitness reports, where you had served, how long you had been in the Navy, how many slots were open and several other things. I wasn't worried about my fitness reports, but my time in service was not long in the grand scope of things. Also, I had heard most of the promotions were going to sailors serving in-country in Vietnam.

"Hear anything yet?" Chief Collins asked.

He had been my mentor, more or less. He is the one who pushed me into taking the test in the first place. I honestly wasn't sure I wanted to make the jump from Petty Officer to Chief. It wasn't a matter of not being able to handle the situation, it was mostly because I didn't like the separation from the men I worked with. As a First-Class Petty Officer, you have a certain comradery. You can hang out with your men, go drinking, and visit foreign ports together. Once you become a Chief, a certain distance must be maintained. They don't usually eat with the regular sailors and they have their own private birthing area. It isn't like they are aloof or thought they were better than the rest of us, but in truth, they were not above pulling rank.

"Nope. Nothing yet. It was my first time taking it. I doubt I'll get the promotion on the first go around."

"It would be pretty unusual. It took me three times before I finally made it. Taking it several times helps add to your score. It's a screwy system, but what can I say, it's the Navy.

I decided to change the subject, "How many sorties do you think they made today?"

"I have no idea but they have been launching around the clock. I understand they are attacking North Vietnam for the most part. Hitting the boat yards," the chief replied.

"We should be using B-52's and pound then into the stone age," I replied.

"I'll pass that along when I'm having dinner with the President next time," the chief retorted.

"Let me run something by you," I said.

"Okay, what ya' got?"

"Well, listen, don't laugh until I finish," I warned.

He got a concerned look and nodded.

"I am thinking about transferring."

He pulled his head back and looked at me like I just told him I had murdered the Captain.

"Wait. You want to do what?" he said.

"I'm playing with the notion of transferring to swift boats or whatever they call them," I replied.

He took a gulp of his coffee before speaking, "Why in the world would you go and do something that stupid? I mean, it's dangerous enough right down here in the engine room without trying to get your ass shot off as well."

"Still, here we are, safe and sound on Yankee Station in the South China Sea, but it's not like what those guys are facing."

"Man, you need to get your head screwed on right. Only a fool would volunteer for that kind of duty. It's one thing when you are told you have to go there, but to volunteer is just plain nuts."

"Look, a lot of other guys are out there fighting. A lot of them volunteered. What makes it so crazy?"

"Duh, getting your butt shot off seems like a pretty good reason to stay right here, safe and sound," the Chief replied.

"I guess I'll make my decision after the results of the Chief Test are announced. If I do make Chief, I'll probably stay right here. If I don't, then I'm going to give serious consideration to applying for the Brown Water Navy," I told him.

He didn't say anything, he just shook his head. I don't know if I would really put in for a transfer but the way I was feeling now, it didn't seem out of the realm of possibility.

***

It was another ten days before the Chief Exam postings were made available. It was pretty much as I had expected. I had passed the test with flying colors but still didn't get the bump in grade. It really bummed me out, but I knew it shouldn't. The chances were slim to none that I would actually make it on the first go around.

I laid in my bunk that night making a mental list of pros and cons of asking for a transfer. I had a Boat Charter Pilot's license from my civilian days and had spent most of my life on the water. I was pretty good mechanically and I could read maps with the best of them. Of course, the downside was the possibility of getting killed. I could come to grips with that. It was getting seriously wounded that bothered me more. Losing my legs or an arm I was not so sure I could hack. I admire people that have gone through something like that and preserver. I don't know if I have the strength to live with a major handicap.

I spent the next week going over and over the rational for even considering a transfer. Was it a death wish? Hero envy? The thrill of danger of risking your life? Geez, what was wrong with me?

On Monday, I told the Chief I was going to talk to the Engineering Officer and ask for a transfer.

"You are really going through with it?"

"Yeah. I've done nothing but think of the pros and cons and I've finally made up my mind."

"Pros and cons? I'll be damned if I can find any pros. This isn't just an adventure. Those little brown gooks are going to try to kill you. They may not know one thing about you, but they know you are the enemy and you are in their country. They want you dead, plain, and simple," the Chief replied.

I said, "You're probably right, but I just feel this is something I need to do."

"Then go. I hope you don't get your dumb ass shot off. Good luck to you."

"Thanks Chief. I'll try to stay in touch," I replied.

"Yeah, sure you will," he said and walked off.

I went and changed to clean dungarees and went to see the Engineering Officer. Major Peters, the Chief Engineering Operations Officer, was a pretty good guy. He left the running of the engine rooms up to us and only came down into the *hole* infrequently to see if we needed any shipyard repairs that we couldn't handle ourselves.

I knocked on his door and he said, "Come."

"Sir, Machinist Mate First Class French requesting a word with you."

He looked at me for a second, took off his reading glasses, placed them on the desk, and said, "Alright French, have a seat and tell me what's on your mind."

I sat down in the chair in front of his desk and collected my thoughts.

"Sir, I would like to put in for a transfer to the Brown Water Navy here in Vietnam."

He looked at me for several seconds before speaking, "You want to go get shot at? Is that what you are asking?"

"Sir, I just think I can better serve my country. Getting a replacement for me in the engine room is easy, but I understand they need boat captains and I already have a Charter Boat Captain's License."

He smiled slightly before saying, "You do realize these aren't party boats or fishing boats? They are war machines and the Viet Cong will be trying to kill you."

"Yes Sir, I am aware of both of those things. I'm just saying that I can handle boats, so I would be a natural for that type of duty."

He leaned back and rubbed his chin. I could almost sense him thinking that I was a total moron for wanting to put myself in the fighting end of the war. Maybe he was right. Maybe I was a moron.

Finally, he said, "You have really thought this through?"

"Yes Sir. That's all I have been thinking about for the last few weeks," I replied.

"Look, once I approve the transfer there is no going back, you do understand that, correct?"

"I do, Sir."

"Alright, I'll sign off on it and send it through the proper channels. It will probably take a few days."

"Thank you, Sir," I said, standing.

"This isn't about getting passed over on the Chief Exam, is it? I saw your name on the list and you did really well on the test. I'm pretty sure you will make it next time."

"No sir, it isn't anything like that. I just want to do more than sit out here doing the same thing day after day."

"Okay, I'll put the paperwork in and you should get your orders in a few days. You should start getting all your gear together."

"Yes sir, I will. Thank you, Sir."

"Thank me? For possible sending you to get shot. You certainly don't have to thank me for that," he replied.

CHAPTER TWO

Eight days later my transfer orders came through. I was both excited and apprehensive. I mean, it is one thing to think about it, but entirely different once you know for sure you are going. I was to present myself to the flight deck with my sea bag and I would be flown to Tan Son Nhat Air Base, Vietnam. The Air Base is located near the main city, Saigon. I was both glad to get off the ship but apprehensive to leave the confines of the USS Ticonderoga.

The other thing I hadn't thought through was how I was going to get to the Son Nhat Air Base. I was hustled aboard an E-2 Hawkeye Command and Control Center twin prop aircraft. There were no luxuries that's for sure. A crewman helped strap me in. I was one of two Navy guys on the flight. One was a third-class radar-man. The other was a Seaman that looked like he was fresh out of boot camp.

We taxied to the launch pad and the plane was hooked to the catapult. I had watched this hundreds of times, but never thought I would be sitting in an aircraft waiting to get shot off the end of an Aircraft Carrier. I had also seen one fail to launch properly and knew if that happened, you were probably not going to survive. I decided to just put that part out of my mind as it was out of my control anyway.

The launch, while like the fastest carnival ride ever invented went off without a hitch and we were air borne in just a few hundred feet and two seconds later. I looked over at the Seaman and saw he was decidedly ten shades whiter than he had been before the launch. The plane was uncomfortable but fortunately, it wasn't a very long flight. The landing was just like any other aircraft landing.

Just about anyone that has been to Vietnam will tell you, two things happen immediately. The superheated blast of hot air instantly causes your clothes to stick to you and almost takes your breath away. The second is the pungent smell of Vietnamese fish-sauce called *núóc-mam*. You mix in the smell of JP fuel, and it almost overwhelms you. I have been in a lot of strange places during my years in the Navy, but this one immediately went to the top of my weird-o-meter.

There were several other military guys standing around waiting for transportation. We were transported by a gray school bus with bars on the window to keep grenades from being tossed in. We were delivered to the in-country processing center. There we were issued jungle fatigues, bonnie hat, helmet, and jungle boots.

I was only there overnight and the next day I was transported via a Huey Helicopter (HU-1). I didn't ask the variant but I understand it was most likely a HU-1D or possibly HU-1H, not that it matters much.

It was my first ride in a chopper and I was more than a little fearful. There were two machine gunners in the open doors. They never took their eyes off the ground. There were four of us being transported. A couple of guys were returning to their units after leaving the hospital. Because of the late start we would be staying over in a place called My Tho. Two of us were NFG's (New F**king Guys) so the pilot decided to scare the crap out of us much to the delight of the veterans.

When we landed I didn't think it was much of a base. It was just some ground scraped clear, some trenches, a bunch of barbed wire surrounding the place, and hundreds of sandbags. Why would anyone even want the place was my first thought? I couldn't see that it was worth much. Instead of leaving the next day, we were held at the base.

For the next two days, the lower ranks (E-3 and below) were sent to do KP duty which I'm sure totally sucked for them. I was happy to be excused from that little detail due to my rank. They also got the shit burning detail.

That is one of the nastier jobs. The toilets empty into cut-off 55-gallon barrels under the toilet seats. They must be pulled out by hand and the contents burned. It's a nasty, but necessary job.

That doesn't mean I had nothing to do. I had to stand guard duty just like everyone else. I was assigned to a watch tower station with two other guys, both Army. They seemed like pretty good guys. They had been in country for three months so they were slowly being accepted by the rest of the squad they had been assigned to. They went on to explain that when they first got here no one wanted to be associated with NFG's. Most of the guy didn't even want to know their names, they just made one up based on some strange criteria.

"Man, they don't even want to be very near you. You are considered fresh meat and you will be dead before the month is out. If you make it two months, they start to accept you. It's frickin' weird," a guy they called Indiana Jones said.

Obviously, he was from Indiana. I wondered if it would be the same with the Navy guys? I assumed I would be assigned to the Brown Water Navy which is what boats that patrol rivers are referred to. Usually, the boats are PBR's (Patrol Boats Ravine) LCS (Combat River Ships) LCU (Cargo Ships) Zippos (Napalm shooters) Monitors, Swifts, and a host of others. I heard there were over a hundred different types of small boats in the Brown Water Navy. Most people think of the river boats as being 'Swift' boats, and yet there is really a myriad of other types that make up the Brown Water Navy. I guess it is just easier to lump them all together.

I was just sort of hanging out, reading a book I had brought with me when all hell broke loose. I could hear, what sounded like, a full-scale attack going on. Later I learned it was just a routine Mike-Mike or Mad Minute where everyone shoots off their weapons to make sure they are working right. Seemed like a hell of a waste of ammo to me but it turned out to be standard operating procedure in the field.

On the second night of duty we started taking mortar rounds. At first, I had no clue what was going on, and then suddenly, the night turned to a sickly day when flairs went off and started drifting down. Everything took on a surreal appearance. Shadows danced and took on an eerie unreal presence. Rounds were being exploded near the fence line and automatic weapon fire began in earnest. It was easy to tell the M16's from the M60's by both the rate of fire and the sound they made. Red and green tracers' cress-crossed back across the void and I could see figures crawling towards the wire. Occasionally, you would see one of the figures suddenly just stop, sprawled out, obviously hit, but others kept coming.

Sappers, which were Viet Cong, would try to blow a hole through the fences so they could over-run the base. They would crawl on their bellies with satchels of explosives. There were a lot more of them than there were of us but we had superior fire power. I had been firing at a group that had managed to make a hole in the fence just a hundred yards from where my guard tower stood. Suddenly, I heard a whistling sound and I dove for the bottom of the guard tower floor. The other two guys just laughed and continued to fire their weapons.

"What?" I shouted, not nearly as amused as they were.

"Man, that's our shit going out. Someone called in an artillery strike," Indiana Jones said and jammed another magazine in his weapon.

If I had stayed standing I would have seen the rounds were landing a good fifty to one hundred yards beyond the fence. A few more rained down on the VC and soon they broke off the attack and faded back into the night. It ended almost as quickly as it started.

Gun fire died down and I could only assume that we must have beaten them back.

"Geez, is it always like that?" I asked.

"Nah, that was pretty tame. They just like to feel us out. It's more of a harassment that an all-out assault They usually do this three or four times a week."

"Yah, but they lose people that way," I argued.

"That is not a gooks major concern. Dinks think dying is a good thing. You need to keep that in mind when you are in the boonies. You give them half a chance and they are likely to kill you. Even if you are trying to save them. As long as they can kill one more American, they will do whatever is necessary."

"Man, that's hard core."

"Dude, they're all hard core. You screw up and give them a chance and you will be going home in a pine box. Only one way to survive out here. You kill them before they can kill you."

I went back to the hooch and some of the others I had come in with were getting back. They were all wide-eyed and giddy. I probably looked the same to them. It was hard to be cool as an NFG in your first firefight.

"Man, that was something," one of them said, plopping down on a cot.

"Frickin' wild man."

"Bodacious," a guy with blond hair added.

"I got one of those gooks. Shot him right in the head. It just exploded," another piped up.

"Shit, I got at least a half dozen," a short little red headed guy said.

Everyone just turned and looked at him. There is always one in every crowd. It didn't seem to faze him that we were looking at him like he was a moron. I figured he was probably used to it. Everyone was pretty hyped up and stories got bigger until around 0400 when we all started to run out of steam.

I had just listened for the most part. I had fired my weapon, but I couldn't say for sure if I hit anyone or not. I had gone through a couple hundred rounds, but did I actually hit anything? I had no real way of knowing.

A few guys were still talking when I laid down and tried to get some sleep. I could hear artillery shells exploding someplace off in the distance. Choppers would take off and land and jets would scream overhead. It took a long time before I finally drifted off. I don't know what time it was, but the sun wasn't up yet when a guy started screaming. We all fumbled around trying to get out of our rack to see what the hell was going on.

We managed to stumble out of our hooch and stood there in our skivvies and boondockers holding our weapons. It turns out that a rat had decided to take a walk across his face and he freaked out. Everyone had a laugh at the NFG and went back to hit the rack.

Rats were a huge problem and they were big, aggressive, and just plain ugly. You could hear them scurrying around in the night and if you shined a light on them they wouldn't bother to run, they just looked at you with those beady luminescent eyes.

It was a hard place to get any real sleep with the constant noise of the 155mm howitzers sending H&I rounds (Harassment and Interdiction) out all night, along with mortar rounds and automatic weapon fire. The M60 Machine Guns would fire off a string of rounds every hour to keep the weapons cleared and ready for use.

I had been issued a Colt M16A1, some called it a widow maker, which was the improved version of those issued earlier in the war. While they weren't as prone to some of the earlier problems I personally thought the AK-47 was a better gun for jungle warfare. I also liked the larger 7.62 x 39 rounds for knock down power. Yah, yah, the 5.56 x 45 tumbles as it goes through a body, but I still thought the AK-47 was an overall better weapon.

When the sun came up I took a tour around the base to see what damage had occurred. I was kind of shocked to see that everything pretty much looked the same. A few more craters here and there but no real damage that I could see. The perimeter wire looked intact so what was the point? Were they just trying to get their men killed?

Speaking of which, I was half expecting to see some dead gooks hanging from the wire or at least lying in the area between the tree line and the base camp. Nothing. Nada. It was almost like nothing ever took place. What a strange way to fight a war.

When I got back to my hooch another new guy was just getting settled in.

"Howdy, I'm Martin French, Machinist Mate First Class," I told him as he dropped his sea bag on the floor between a couple of cots.

"PFC Norman Gills," he said without offering to shake hands.

"Just get in today?"

"Yah, this place sucks already."

"Hey, it gets worse," I replied.

"I doubt it," Gills said.

He was a frail looking guy with wire rimmed glasses. He didn't look particularly fit and I wondered how he had got sent here. He certainly was no jock that was for sure.

"Know where you are headed yet?"

"Some shit hole called An Khe," he replied.

"Don't know it. I just got here two days ago. Three now I guess."

"What is a Navy guy doing here?" he asked.

"We have boats all up and down the rivers. I guess I'll be going to one of them," I told him.

"I mean, why are you here? The Navy had ships all over the world. How did you get sent to this scumbag place?" he asked.

"Ah. Actually, I volunteered. I wanted to see what all the fuss was about. What you read in the news and see on television is scripted. I wanted to find out for myself what it was really like.

He looked at me for a moment trying to decide if I was putting him on or not. When I didn't smile or laugh he just slowly shook his head.

"Man, you are seriously f***ed up."

That was the last time I spoke to him. Not because of what he had said, but because my orders came in and I packed and was off to my new duty station.

CHAPTER THREE

This time I wasn't quite as nervous about climbing onboard the Huey. The door gunner showed me how to 'look cool' by hanging your leg on the skids with your weapon pointed down. Well, by all means, I wanted to look cool when I reported to my new duty station.

It wasn't much of a hop to Vĩnh Long which would become my home for the next year. The pilot dropped me off at the air strip. I was surprised that they had sent a jeep to pick me up. It looked like it was left over from WWII and was painted a dull olive color. The only thing that was lacking was the big white star they put on them during WWII.

The driver was EM 3 (Electricians Mate third-class) James Hall. He informed me he was known as Jimbo. Okay then.

"Throw your shit in the back and let's haul," he said, and I did exactly that and climbed in beside him.

I had a thousand questions I wanted to ask him but I decided to let him talk and try to keep up with the flow of the conversation.

"Where you from?" he asked.

"Georgia."

"No shit? Reds from Georgia. What part?"

"Marietta."

"Never heard of it."

"It's just outside of Atlanta," I explained.

He shrugged and said, "Okay. If you say so."

He was driving at a breakneck speed. Dust was flying out like a vapor trail behind us. I wondered if we were late for something.

"Yah, I know what you're thinking. Why is Jimbo driving like a maniac? Well, the slope heads have been acting up lately. I don't want them to get a pot shot at me. Them dinks are pretty good shots," he said, taking a corner that made me grab the windshield frame.

We bounced over the rough terrain and across a couple of old rickety bridges that I wasn't too sure about. Five minutes later we slid to a halt inside the compound.

"Come on. Grab your shit. I'll show you where to check-in," he said and started off.

The structure was nothing more than a bunch of sandbags stacked up with wood for a ceiling and more sandbags on top along with a liner over it to keep rain out. Sitting behind a desk made of ammo crates and a sheet of plywood was a clean-shaven guy, that I took to be in charge. He had no rank on and nothing on his desk indicated it, but he looked the part.

I saluted and said, "Machinist Mate First Class, Martin French reporting as ordered."

"Ah, have a seat and take a load off. I'm Lieutenant Ellis. Glad to have you aboard. Welcome to IV Corps. A few days later and you would have had a much steeper learning curve. As it is, you will have a couple of days with MM1 Tiller, whom you are replacing. Being the new guy, don't expect too much from your crew until they see how you fit in. Out here things are a little different. More...relaxed in some ways and a lot more tense in others. Speaking of which, that is the last time you will salute me. It gives the gooks a possible target."

"Sorry, I didn't know," I replied.

"Don't worry about it. Just keep it in mind. Now, I know you have a hundred questions, but I will take you down to your boat and introduce you to your crew. You can leave your sea bag here until we get you situated," he told me and stood up.

He had my file and I assumed he knew I had been through weapons training and knew that I had worked as an OUVP/Six-Pack licensed fishing charter boat captain in Georgia.

When he stood, he was taller than I had realized. I guess he had been sitting on an upended crate and that made him look shorter. As it was, his head hit the top of the structure. Granted it wasn't all that big but he was a little over six-foot tall, with gray hair at the temples, and liquid brown eyes.

"So, they told me you volunteered for this duty," he said while we were walking along.

"Yes sir."

"Why?"

"I don't have a firm reason. I guess I just wanted to see what this war was really all about. What you see on the television is kind of fake. I wanted to find out for myself."

We walked in silence for a few seconds before he said, "Son, you are in for a hell of a shock. Everyone that comes here leaves differently than when they arrived. You are going to see and do things you thought you would never do. It's war, and our only job here is to kill ol' Charlie before he blows our ass away. We don't give warnings, none of that 'Stop or I'll shoot crap'. You shoot first and then you can say stop. If you don't, you'll be dead within a week. You need to understand that. Yes, there are rules of engagement, but frankly those are for the politicians back home. Their ass isn't on the line. Out here we pretty much blast everything that moves. Just keep that in mind when you go out on patrol."

Well, okay then. That seemed kind of harsh, and I wondered if he really meant all of that, or it was a standard spiel he gave to all NFG's. We walked out on this short concrete pier and I saw six boats lashed together. A little further back another one was being lifted out of the water.

"These are PBR boats. In the usual Naval parlance, Patrol Boat, Riverine. They are made of fiberglass and have two Detroit Diesel engines that produce around two hundred and twenty horsepower each. They are coupled to a jet drive system. The MKII that you will be taking over is thirty-two feet long and has a beam of eleven and a half feet. These things can operate in two feet of water so they are perfect for the job we do here."

"But no armor to protect the boat?'

"None to speak of. They rely on speed and maneuverability. That, along with some pretty serious fire power. Your boat has two 50 cal. machine guns in the bow and a single 50 cal. on the stern. It has two 7.62 light machine guns, one on each side along with a 40mm grenade launcher. It can hold its own against most things," he told me.

Easy for him to say. I would imagine an RPG would do a hell of a lot of damage. My boat was the first one tied up next to the pier. Four guys in ragged fatigues were standing on the boat. Two of them had cut off the legs of the pants to make shorts. All had cut the arms off the shirts. One had on a flak jacket. None of them stood when the LT and I stepped on board.

"Listen up men. This is MM1 Martin French. Ya all know Tilly is out of here in a couple of days..."

"Two days, nine hours and...." he said looking at his watch, "twenty-seven minutes."

"Right, anyway, French will be the new boat Captain. This here is," he pointed to a thin, tanned guy with brown eyes, brown hair, and a thin mustache, "EM 2 Dalton Lake. Goes by 'Sketter'. He is your engine guy. The ugly one next to him looking half asleep is Gunners Mate 2, Donald Fowler. He answers to 'Quacker'. Just don't call him Donald Duck. He gets real pissed when he is called that. Finally, as you might guess, is seaman 'Tex', James Rigger. I guess his hat kind of gives him away. He is from Texas and will remind you of that every chance he gets. If he could keep out of trouble long enough he would be a third-class petty officer, but it just doesn't seem to be in his bones," the LT said.

They nodded or grunted. Quacker gave me a peace sign which I returned.

"You are now officially the boat Captain of PBR 991, part of the five-two river division. I'll show you to your hooch and you can settle in," the LT offered.

"I'll do it," Tiller, a tall, skinny black man said, jumping up on the dock.

"Good. I have some paperwork to take care of. Stop by the CP before you go back to the boat," LT Ellis said, as we parted.

"Well bro, you are officially up shit creek without a paddle," Tiller said, as we walked along the dusty path.

"Is it all that bad?" I asked.

"Not if you don't mind dying for a living. Out here you never know when an attack is coming. You can be cruising along, the sun is out, and all seems right with the world. Then out of nowhere the SHTF and you are in a world of hurt. One piece of advice. Never. Never. Ever let your guard down, and don't let your men jack around when you are on patrol. Tied up at the pier, let them have at it, but once those engines start, it should be all business. They are going to test you to see what they can get away with. Kind of like a substitute teacher. You don't need to jump down their throats. A good hard look or some indication that you know what they are up to usually gets the job done. They may be my brothers, but I won't hesitate to kick them in the ass if they goof off on patrol."

When we got to the hooch I was going to be assigned to, I put my stuff away in the footlocker at the end of the cot. I made a quick check for rats but didn't see any. Of course, it was still day, so night would be an entirely different situation.

While I was putting my stuff away we talked about the PBR's maneuvering ability, draft at speed, which was just a few inches, and what to check before heading out. It was pretty obvious he knew his job.

"Don't worry about all of this. After you talk to the LT we will go down and take her out for a spin. You will get a better feel for what I'm talking about. You have driven a boat before, right?"

"Heck no," I said.

He looked at me with his eyes bugging out.

"Just kidding. Yeah, I've been around boats all my life. I rented a 40-footer to cruise the intercostal water ways in Florida a couple of times. I also operated a 64ft charter fishing boat in Atlanta," I told him.

"Damn, you about made me piss my pants for a second. Okay, if you're done, let's get over to see the LT so I can get you out on the water," Teller said.

"Let's do it."

CHAPTER FOUR

"Any questions?" the LT said after we had talked for almost an hour.

"Not that I can think of at the moment. Tiller is going to take the boat out and let me get the feel of it."

"Excellent. If you think of anything, feel free to stop by. Welcome to the Brown Water Navy."

"Thank you LT"

I walked down to the boat and saw that Tiller had the crew all in flak jackets and pants. When I stepped on board 'Tex' untied us from the other boats and pier and stood waiting to throw the lines off.

"Okay. First when we have time, like now, we do a pre-check. Just like pilots do on planes. It's just a quick check to make sure everything is shipshape. Skeeter checks the engines to make sure they are ready to go. Quacker checks all the weapons to ensure that they are locked and loaded and ready to go. That includes the shotguns, M-16's and M60's. The last thing you want is to grab a weapon and not have it ready to fire. He also checks the ammo inventory for everything we have on board. The only thing he doesn't check is your personal sidearm. Hopefully, you are smart enough to do that. I like to do a radio check before I even start the engines. It's pretty simple. You will be assigned a call code. The LT is Coastal One.

He picked up the mic, keyed it and said, "Costal One, this is Costal Three. We are heading out for an indoctrination run."

"Rodger three. Proceed as planned."

"Okay, that's done, so now I test the controls. The jets are connected to the steering wheel by cables. It doesn't take much to change headings. Think of it as a sports car. A little input equals a lot of change. These are the two throttles. These two levers control the U-gates that stop or reverse the boat. If you have driven twin engine boats you probably know what most of the gauges are for. Tachometers, one for each engine, oil pressure of each engine, water temp gauges, fuel gauges, batteries. Hell, you can figure them out. Probably the one thing that might be different is the Raytheon 1900N radar. I'll turn it on and when we get out a little way, I'll show how it works. Everyone, at your stations," he called out.

"I've used a similar Raytheon before on my charter boat," I said.

"Far out."

Tex threw the line in the boat and jumped in. Quaker took up his position on the twin 50's up front while Tex manned the stern 50 cal. Skeeter stood beside me in the cockpit leaning on the metal plate that held the 7.62 machine gun.

He pushed the buttons and the engines roared to life. He took a quick look around and eased the boat out of the slip.

"Okay. I'm going to show you what the boat is capable of then I am going to have you do it. Don't worry about getting it right the first time. I was lousy at first. It's like everything else, you should become one with the boat and trust in what it can do. A lot of what they teach you in school is crap. They don't tell the real story," Tiller said.

We eased out a few hundred yards towards the middle of the river before he told me to hang on.

"Peddle to the medal boys," he shouted and then looked over at me, "Don't be a hero, grab on to something."

I grabbed on to the stanchion and held on tight. He shoved the two levers forward until they couldn't go any further. The boat shot up and was on plane before I could even say 'Wow'. The thing was like a water rocket. Within seconds we were flat out with most of the boat out of the water, or so it seemed.

"Geez. Nothing like the boats I have driven. Nothing comes even close," I shouted.

"It can flat haul ass in no time. Gets your ass out of trouble PDQ," Teller replied, "Hang on, you haven't seen anything."

He threw the reversing handles full down and the bow of the boat plunged down into the water causing it to break over the bow. At almost the same time he turned the wheel hard left and brought the right reversing lever up again. The boat practically pivoted on itself while he brought the other lever up. Within seconds we were panned out, heading 180 degrees from our previous course.

"Holy crap," I finally was able to get out.

I had never seen anything like that before. My boats had never done anything like that either.

"Impressive huh?" Tiller said.

"Un-frickin'-believable."

He did a series of abrupt direction changes and I simply couldn't believe the maneuverability of the PBR.

"Okay. I'm going to show you how to approach a sampan for inspection," he said pointing to two small boats a few hundred yards ahead.

"The first thing you look for is if they suddenly change directions and try to run. If they do, it almost always means they are carrying something they shouldn't be. Ammo, arms, munitions, or they don't have the proper papers," he told me.

"How do you know what they have or if the papers are in order?"

"This time we will just search the sampans. When we are on this kind of patrol we often have a civilian Viennese MP on board who does that part."

He maneuvered the boat over to where one of the sampans was now stopped. He reversed and brought the PBR to a halt. Tex went over to the side with the sampans and secured them to the PBR. Tiller had his M16 slightly pointed at the boat. He didn't take his eyes off them. Skeeter appeared with his M16 ready as well.

Obviously, they had seen a routine stop go to hell on more than one occasion. I watched the precision in which the crew went about the checks. Tex got on one boat and started looking around. There was a mound of rice in the first sampan. He stirred through it several times to make sure nothing was hidden. Satisfied he got back on the boat. Tiller handed the Vietnamese a couple packs of cigarettes. Everyone lit up and they seemed none too put out and off they went.

"You never take your eyes off them. Not even for a second. You have to watch their eyes and mannerisms. If they start fidgeting, it usually means they are up to no good. Not always, but you need to be ready just in case. We have had to blow a couple out of the water while they were right alongside us. If they make an aggressive move, don't think, just start blowing them away. They are most likely VC. My men are my only concern in a situation like that. That extends to kids as well. One of our boats got pretty well blown to hell when the two kids with the parents lobbed grenades into one of our boat. We had one KIA and two WIA. You don't want that to happen to your men," he said sternly.

I understood where he was coming from, but I didn't know about shooting a kid. I mean the VC yeah, but a kid? They were only doing what they were told or forced to do. I really didn't know if I could do such a thing.

We went through the drill of stopping sampans a couple of more times and I started focusing on the actions and faces of the Vietnamese. Some seemed friendly and others were somewhat hostile, but they were smart enough to know there was little they could do about it.

"Okay, you take over, I'll tell you what to do. Let's just get the feel of the boat before you get into the more difficult stuff," Tiller told me and stepped away from the console.

I put my hand on the wheel and rested my other on the throttles like I had seen him do. I kept it straight and quickly glanced at the gauges. We were cruising along around 30 knots in water as smooth as glass. It reminded me of the early mornings when I would go out on the lake and water skiing before all the crazies got up and ruined the tranquility.

Tiller had me go through a few easy maneuvers to get the feel of the PBR. He had me start and stop under normal conditions a bunch of times. He showed me how the U-tubs worked and how they helped control the boat during tight turns. I was pretty bad at it I'll admit. To him it was natural, I struggled to get it right every time. I didn't know what the crew thought and I doubt I really wanted too.

As the sun got lower, we continued to do various drills and maneuvers. He had picked up the pace in his orders. Just to complicate my concentration he had the gun's fire while I was trying to remember how to do the various drills.

"Stop, stop," he suddenly yelled.

I pulled the throttles back quickly but the wake caught up with the stern and shoved us a good hundred yards further on.

"Well, congratulations. You just killed your entire crew and blew the boat to hell," he said.

"I didn't reverse the thrust," I said shaking my head.

"That's right. In an emergency, you must know how to get the boat stopped in the shortest distance. If we had been rolling into an ambush they would have kicked your butt. The gooks are good at reacting quickly. You would have been picking splinters out of your ass from an RPG, if you survived.

For the next hour, I did nothing but emergency turnarounds and fast stops. I was starting to get the hang of it. I still had to think about it, but at least I was better. We stopped a few more sampans and I did what he had done previously, immediately got my M16 at the ready and watched the Vietnamese faces and body language.

Once the sun went down, it got dark real fast. It had been easy to see during the daylight hours, but now I could hardly make out anything.

"You need to rely on the Raytheon radar screen. It will tell you what's around you. What it doesn't help with, is dinks waiting in ambush ready to smoke your sorry ass."

"So, what do you do about that?" I asked.

"You hone your senses. You keep your men sharp and you get ready to bugout the moment the first shot is fired. It's hard to spot them at night. We are often backlit by the moon so they can see us better than we can see them. Once they open fire you can pinpoint them, but honestly, I doubt much damage is done by either side. We just blast away until they either stop or they are getting zeroed in on us. Live to fight another day is my motto," Tiller said.

"But what if it is a large force. Don't we need to stop them," I asked.

"That's what the choppers are for. We have two slicks assigned to us. We call in the position and they scramble the birds. They come sweeping and unload with mini-guns and rockets. We just stay on station and continue to fire at the gooks. Typically, once the flyboys show up, they bug out of the area."

I glanced at my watch and Tiller saw me and said, "We operate on twelve-hour shifts. Usually two boats go out. Where they go is determined at a meeting held in the CP. Sometimes by Matt Pierce, senior enlisted man. Matt's good people and knows what he is talking about. He takes his job seriously. This is his second tour."

"What about the LT?" I said.

"Not bad. He is smart enough to defer to Matt when a dangerous call has to be made. He doesn't let his ego get in the way. He tries to take care of his men and doesn't let them get in over their heads if he can help it. I guess the best thing I can say is that I trust him. Unfortunately for you, he only has five more months before he rotates out of here."

"What about Matt?" I asked.

"Not sure. Maybe two months at most. They will either replace him with someone new or if he stays for a third tour, he may get to stay here," Tiller replied.

"Well, all of that's down the road. For now, I just need to concentrate on operating the boat and staying out of trouble."

"Got that right," he said.

We continued to work on my skills and reaction times to his commands. I got better at reading the radar screen and handling the radio. I called in routine sit-reps each hour and passed along other information.

"This is about the time that the crew's eyes start to get heavy. You need to make sure they are alert. I sometimes stop the boat and make everyone get up and stretch for a minute or so. They grumble, but it's better than someone falling asleep and putting everyone in danger," Tiller advised me.

It was almost 0100 before we got back to the docks. Once the ship was secured we headed to our hooch to grab some z's. My mind was crammed full and it took me a little while to unwind and fall asleep. I did learn that Tex and Quacker snored like pigs rooting for food.

CHAPTER FIVE

The LT had called a meeting for 10:00 a.m. the following morning. We ate as a crew and all went to the CP at the prescribed time. There were more people than I expected.

"Sorry, I forgot to mention, we go out in teams of two usually, but obviously something bigger is going on," Tiller said when he saw me looking around.

"Ah," was all I said.

It made sense when you thought about it. If something happened and you were all alone it would be very bad indeed. Even something as simple as an engine malfunction. In pairs, at least you could get towed back. But this many crews indicated that indeed something big was happening.

"Alright, let's start. Last night new intel from CIC was passed along to us. It seems the VC have moved a lot of bodies and munitions into our area of operation," Matt told us.

Matt pointed to a map set up on an easel that was large enough for us all to see without out having to crowd around. He used his finger to point to an area upriver.

"This is us, and this is where our intel says they have set up," he said pointing to a place called Cao Lahn, "There is a place where the river splits around an island. They have set up an ambush anvil sight to protect the troops and munitions a few hundred yards further up the river at this point, Ben do An Nhon. According to the information we got, they estimate between one hundred and two hundred are at the ambush point. A heck of a lot more are further upstream. Because of that we will be combining forces with a couple of swift boats, two Alpha boats and four LCI's. Our AO is the ambush sight. Air Cav, fastmovers, mostly F-100 and F-4's, along with dime-nickels will be CAS attack mode on the main force. While all of this is going on, a third blocking force will be above An Nhon if they try to exfil. You will have two slicks that will be available if you need them. Don't be afraid to call them in and don't wait until the last minute. Look guys, this is going to be an asskicker but you should be okay if you use your heads and work as a team. No heroics or trying to outdo the other guys. We will be break-squelch only if an emergency arises. Make sure all your maps are up to date and everyone is battle ready. Everyone needs to have their head screwed on right. Now, I want the boat captains to remain, the rest of you go get extra ammo and whatever else you need," he said.

Matt waited until they were all gone except for the six of us that were the captains. We all moved in closer and he had us take a knee.

"Guys, I ain't gonna shit you one little bit. I'm not sure how well this whole operation was thought out. If the ambush guys are loaded down with B-40's you are going to have quite a time on your hands just dodging the damn things. I also think they downplayed how many troops are involved in the ambush. I think there will be more there and at the secondary site. I'm serious about not being heroes. Engage the gooks but don't get sucked in. They may well let the first two boats pass before they spring the trap. Just be on the lookout. I'll tell you another thing that is bothering me. It is very narrow there and they could have put a second trap on the island. You would be caught up in a crossfire and that is deadly. I want you six to discuss how to proceed upriver and how to handle the attack. I won't be there so you guys have to use your own discretion. Also, keep in mind that the swift boat captains think they are superior to our PBR's so if they want to charge ahead, let them. That's about it, any questions?"

Just a few hundred I thought but since no one else spoke up, neither did I. The last thing he did was give us the radio frequencies and code words we would need during the mission.

"Tiller and French. Hang on a second," Matt said as everyone was filing out.

"First, nice to meet you French, Tiller says you are a fast learner. That's a good thing. This is a hell of a mission to throw at you right off the bat but it can't be helped. You need to let the others take the lead and watch what they do and how they work together. No John Wayne stuff."

"That isn't a problem. I'm smart enough to know my limits and the last thing I want to do is put my men in jeopardy. Besides, I'm sure Tiller will keep me under control," I answered.

"Tiller won't be going along. He has a wake-up and then he is gone. No way I am letting him go out on this mission. You have good men; they know what to do. Your slot will be the sixth PBR on this op," Matt told me.

"I understand," I replied.

He nodded his head and we departed. This was a hell of a time to find out I would be doing this on my own. Thrown into a major battle with no experience in a firefight seemed like a disaster waiting to happen. Another SNAFU if ever there was one.

"I guess I thought you already realized that," Tiller said as we were walking down to the boat.

"Honestly, it never entered my mine. I've been concentrating on the boat so much I just didn't put two and two together. I mean it makes sense."

"Look man, I would go with you but I'm so short. I don't have time for a long conversation. I could walk under the belly of a snake," Tiller replied.

"I get it. Hell, I wouldn't go if it was me either."

"Just let the crew do their job and everything will be fine. Keep an eye on the other boats joining us. We have never worked with them before so I can't tell you what to expect. Our guys will be fine. They will look out for you."

"I'll do that," I replied.

"I mean it. The reputation of the Swift Boat operators is they think they are the only real brown water navy sailors. They tend to look down on PBR drivers."

"I'll keep that in mind," I said as we reached the dock.

"Good luck to you. No fancy stuff. Just get this one under your belt," were Tiller's parting words.

He waved, turned, and walked back up the path to pack his stuff. He never looked back once. He would be long gone by the time we came back. I was surprised he didn't go on the boat and tell the guys goodbye. I guess that was the way it was at the end of a tour. It did seem strange, nevertheless.

When I got on the boat, only Tex said, "Tiller's gone, right?"

"As we speak," I told him.

That's all he said and went about helping 'Quacker' load extra ammo and two M-79 grenade launchers. I wondered where they had gotten them but decided not to ask.

Most of the rest of the day was kind of a waste. All the boats were tied up getting ready for the arrival of the remainder of the task force. I spent the day with the crew just shooting the shit, listening to their war stories, and fighting off mosquitoes. The mosquitoes are like a pack of hungry vultures. They come in thousands and towards evening they swarm in a dark cloud. You can bathe in mosquito repellent but all it seems to do is to make them hungrier.

I didn't say much, I just let them do the talking. If all of it was true they had pretty much been through the grinder. All sailors like to embellish stories but these seemed pretty accurate. As suspected and predictable, I became known as Frenchie. It wasn't the first time I had been tagged with that name. Let's face it with a last name like French what else are they going to call me?

We had eaten C-rations for lunch on the boat but now dusk was closing in and we decided to go get a hot meal. A slick had brought in hot food from an LCT further down river. While the food wasn't all that good, it was hot and a heck of a lot better than the C-rats we had consumed at noon.

The sun had just set when we heard the sound of boats coming upriver. A few minutes later two aluminum hulled swift boats, the Alpha boats, and the LCI's came into view. They maneuvered close to our boats and they tied up fore and aft of ours. After everyone had scrambled ashore we introduced ourselves and headed for the CP.

LT Ellis told us that Captain Stills would be arriving within the hour to go over the battle plan. That seemed kind of redundent to me. We all knew what the target was and who was doing what. Why we needed another briefing was beyond me.

The LT pulled the PBR crews aside and told us to just look interested and not ask questions. This was for show so the Captain could get credit for the operation if it went as expected. If not, he would somehow blame it on someone else, probably the LT.

Ah, the old CYA even out here in the boonies. Career officers always wanted to be associated with the successes and disenfranchised from the failures. We could hear the slick coming up the river and then it popped over the tree line and started its descent. Dust, small branches, and rocks were thrown out from the rotor blades until the pilot shut the chopper down.

A tall thin man with almost totally white hair and a white mustache hopped out of the chopper and made his way over to the LT. The two men exchanged salutes and Ellis stood talking to him for a minute before they came over to where we had all assembled.

"Gather around me," he said in a voice that seemed full of vim and vigor.

"Gentlemen, this operation is a precursor of an even larger operation we are planning. The official name of our mission starting tomorrow is 'Big Sting'. We want to eliminate the choke hold the VC have placed at Cao Lahn. We want to further destroy the enemy at An Nhon. This is a test to see if the swifts, PBR's, Alphas, and LCI can work as a team. I know it will be a difficult assignment but it is a vital one for the planning of future operations. The Big Sting is also the means by which we hope to cut off the flow of goods down the Ho-Chi-Min Trail. It is vital that we cut the supplies going into South Vietnam. The plan calls for the swifts to lead the way up the river, then the PBR's followed by the Alpha boats, and then the LCI's to land men ashore to perform a S & D of the area. Once the Search and Destroy mission is accomplished, the men then re-board the LCI's and head up to An Nhon to lend assistance as needed. As many of you know, the latest intel has the Cong on both sides of the Cao Lahn ambush so you need to be ready on both sides of the river."

He blathered on for another ten minutes basically just listening to himself talk. We all knew what was waiting for us, we just wanted to get on with the mission. The only bit of new news was that we had an official operation name; Big Sting, and that other attacks using a composite of boats was planned. Putting grunts ashore after an attack had not been done in our sector before. Tex said that they had dropped off LRP's and Special Forces units but nothing on this scale. I guess the Brown Water Navy was going to take on a new role. Far out, and I'm getting thrown into it without having any experience.

CHAPTER SIX

The operation kicked off at 0230 as all the boats fired up their engines. Mine was the last PBR to leave the dock. I was to trail behind three hundred yards from the boat in front of me until we got to a point just below the ambush site. It was a dark night with just a sliver of a waxing moon. The Song Tien river was as smooth as glass as we traveled along at fifteen knots which is just a tad over seventeen miles per hour. We could go no faster than the slowest LCI or the attack would not be coordinated.

Pha Cao Lanh was a small fishing village on the port bank. We were all to stop there and make sure everyone was together and ready. One of the two Alpha boats had been having radar problems but traveling in a pack like this would not make it much of a problem. Someone in the lead would have spotted any boats up ahead.

It was 0545 when everyone was finally ready. We all made our final crosscheck before heading out. Our attack was to be just at first light, which would give us a full ten hours of sunlight. The Swifts moved out first and off we went. We had separated a little more to allow for more maneuvering room. I was about five hundred yards behind the fifth boat in line.

When we got to the ambush point at 0645 the first boat went through the divide and no shots were fired. The second boat had lagged and when it followed through, the starboard bank immediately opened up. The other PBR went to full power and soon we were all firing at the shoreline. As I swung my boat around the other side of the bank opened fire and I could hear small arms bullets hitting the hull of the boat. I thrust it into reverse and backed down, stopped for just a second, and then floored it. It caught them off guard and we slipped out of the ambush. By now the Alpha boats and swifts had joined in and we were pounding both sides of the river. Skeeter was using one of the M79's to lob grenades. Quacker was yelling at the top of his lungs as he blasted the shoreline with the twin 50's. Tex was shooting over at the other side on the second ambush sight.

A bullet ricocheted off the stanchion that held the radar, close enough for me to hear the buzz of the bullet. Up until that moment I had been too busy working the controls, dodging the other boats, and trying to keep a reasonable distance from the shore. Bullets were splashing in the water all around the boat and at times I wondered why we were still afloat.

The VC were firing B-40 RPG's with HEAT warheads left and right. Three crossed right over the top of our boat and one landed just a few yards in front of us. One of the Alpha boats took a hit on the bow section. The boat seemed to lift for a moment and I saw two men get thrown over the side. There was no way to know if they were alive or dead. The Alpha boat rides a little deeper in the water than the PBR and when it started to turn I could see a large section of the front of the boat was missing. Water was sloshing up and into the hull breach. The other Alpha boat broke off the attack immediately and went full throttle over to help the wounded vessel. Two of the PBR's from our group went to render aid in the form of a shield, trying to keep the VC from zeroing in on the vessel.

I made a sharp starboard turn and joined them, pounding the shoreline with everything we had. What we needed was a zippo but none had been assigned to our detail.

The swift boats weren't very effective in the narrow confines where we were fighting. They are less maneuverable and had a harder time turning to make another run. The PBR's could do a 180 degree turn in just a few feet making them ideal for this environment. To be fair, the swifts were designed to be used along the coast and larger water ways and this was a real stretch of their ability. They fought valiantly but the number of passes they made were about a third of the PBR's and Alpha boats.

Just as things were starting to quiet down an RPG came screaming out of nowhere from the island side of the ambush. I just caught it out of the corner of my eye at the same time Tex yelled 'RPG, port side'.

I immediately turned towards the missile and headed off at a slight angle. The rocket zoomed by, missing us by inches and landing in the water by our stern. It exploded, sending a cascade of water raining down on us. Tex opened up on the spot it came from and that was the last rocket to come from that area. Finally, the LCI' that had been hanging back, hit the shore and the grunts disembarked to start the S & D (Search & Destroy) part of the mission.

You could hear the firefight raging as the grunts were perusing the VC as they tried to escape. The slower heavier sounds of the AK-47 versus the lighter sound, faster cycling M16 could pretty much tell you who was winning. The AK-47 began to diminish in volume and eventually stopped all together.

At this point we were pretty much finished with our part. The grunts were too far inland for us to offer much support but we stayed on station just in case everything went south. I edged our boat over to the Alpha boat that had been hit with the RPG. It was starting to list to the starboard side and I could see where a large chunk of the bow was missing. Two men were laying on deck, obviously dead. One was missing his right arm and leg and the other had a large stomach wound.

It wasn't until this point that I realized how quickly you could die. I mean, one moment they were firing away at the shore and the next they were blown to bits. As you would expect, the guys on the Alpha were glum and just going about their duties on autopilot.

One of the swift boats was tied up to the stricken vessel and they had run a line over that was attached to a pump to try to keep the boat afloat. It was helping but I seriously doubted that once underway they could make it back to the docks. I knew the Alphas were tough little boogers but I simply didn't see how it could make it that far afloat.

It was going on 1600 before the grunts returned and boarded the LCI's. They carried four guys on makeshift stretchers and I assume they had called in for a dust off because I could hear the sound of a slick's rotors making its way up the river. A few minutes later it came into sight and landed in a small clearing at the edge of the water.

The four men were rushed over and quickly tossed into the Medevac Huey. A few seconds later it was airborne and heading back the way it had come. With the swift boat on one side and my boat on the other, we tied off the Alpha boat and decided we would try our best to get it back to the jump off point. It was time to book, so we headed out into the river.

The other boats fell in behind us and we started home. We could only go a few knots or else the bow would plow under, taking on even more water. We were about halfway back when the boat started to get even deeper in the water. My boat was listing to the port side as it pulled me over as well. The Swift boat was fairing a little better but it was obvious that it was struggling as well.

Finally, we came to the realization that it was a futile effort and that we were simply not going to be able to save her. We pulled her over near the shore. Part of the crew climbed on to the Alpha and we gathered up the dead crew members. The captain of the stricken boat was busy busting up the radar unit and the radio. He stripped everything he could off the boat before finally abandoning it. We released the lines and stood by waiting for it to sink.

"You might want to beat feet. I placed some C-4 with a det cord," he told us.

That was good enough for me and I floored the throttles and we were about thirty yards away when the explosion went off. The Alpha jumped up in the air, almost out of the water and then immediately began to sink. I stopped the engines and we all sat there watching the boat die. No navy guy likes to see any boat or ship sink unless it is the enemies.

By the time we left you could no longer see the whip antenna sticking out of the water. I had half expected it to only sink to the cabin line but evidently it was deeper there than many other places. We made our way back to base and moored the ships like previously, minus the one Alpha boat. Needless to say, we were all pretty bummed out. Four grunts KIA or WIA and two sailors KIA. Bad vibes for sure.

LT Ellis was there to meet us. His foot was resting on a big red and white cooler. He waited for us all to gather around. The LT expressed his sorrow at the loss of the Alpha boat and the two crew members. He said that he wanted to pass on from Captain Stills, congratulations on a job well done. He was saddened to learn of the loss of the two crew members and the Alpha boat but that we had kicked Charlies butt good and proper. He then opened the cooler and it was crammed full of Schlitz beer in ice. No one could believe there was actually cold beer, in bottles. Everyone was used to drinking the rotgut warm and mostly out of cans. It didn't take long for all the beers to be passed around.

Tex, Skeeter, and Quacker all told me this was an absolute first. To their knowledge it had never been done before. LT's reputation took a huge leap. How he had done it was a mystery but that night it helped everyone to let their hair down.

Later, I wrote out my combat after action report. I wasn't sure how you condensed all the action down to a page. So much had happened. I finally wrote:

COMBAT AFTER ACTION REPORT: Martin French; MM1

GENERAL: Action consisted of the following: Six (6) PBR's; Two (2) Alpha Boats; Two (2) Swift Boats; Two (2) LCI with 24 Army Infantry Personal.

MISSION: Acting on intelligence reports of an ambush at a choke point on the Tien River. Ambush was reported to be near Cao Lahn where the river splits. To clear the ambush sight and destroy any munitions found at said location.

WEATHER: 0230 sky clear with no rain. Sun rise at 0551 with clear skies.

COMBAT REPORT: In contact with enemy at 0645. The enemy held fire until the second Swift passed the choke point and they opened fire with AK-47's; RPG's; light machine guns. Fire was immediately retuned and evasive action was undertaken by all boats. The fire fight lasted for approximately fifty-five (55) minutes before the LCI's could unload the infantry. They immediately initiated a Search and Destroy mission. We held on station to cover the LCI's until the infantry completed their mission. Secondary explosions were due to munitions destruction.

KIA: Terry Wilson EM2

James Thomas SM

WIA: Stan Ham

Nate Liston

Ben Collins

Ralph Keller

Robert Dillon

Samuel English

EQUIPMENT LOST:

ALPHA BOAT (S114)

MM1 Martin French

I submitted it to LT Ellis and waited while he read it.

"First after-action report," he said as a statement, so I just waited.

"Overall, not too bad. You are missing some details but I must say, you're the first one to turn in a report. I usually have to kick ass to get the others to write up their reports."

"At least I got something right," I said.

He rummaged through a filing cabinet and pulled out a folder. He brought it over to his desk and looked through it until he found what he was looking for. He pulled out a sheet of paper and handed it over to me.

"Follow this format and you won't have any problems," he told me.

I thanked him and took the paper along with my report and made the corrections immediately and returned it to him.

"Damn French, I didn't mean you had to do it right this minute but I appreciate it. Go get some sack time. We are sending no boats out tonight," he said.

"Thank you, sir," I said and almost saluted before I caught myself.

I went back to the hooch and found that everyone was already racked out and copping Z's. I joined them in minutes.

CHAPTER SEVEN

The next day we spent the morning making repairs to the boats. Some were in worse condition that others. The other boats that had joined us had already departed back to their own bases.

I was surprised at how many hits we had taken. Two or three had hit the plates the protect the cabin. I hadn't even heard them in the heat of battle. A little fiberglass here and some paint and the PBR was ready to go again.

Our next mission was back to routine patrol. A Vietnamese cop came to the docks and got on board. He would be the one checking papers and documents. Ours and PBR 913 headed out. We were following because while I had been onboard almost a week I had still not done a routine patrol. We headed out at 1200 hours and immediately started stopping sampans.

Man, the cop was rough. Giấy tờ, Giấy tờ, he would shout at them. He did a lot of yelling and seemed impatient. Once he got all the ID's and paperwork he would hold them until we had gotten a man on board and checked out the cargo. Most of the time it was people on their way to market. Rice was by far the largest amount of goods moved.

The day passed quickly since there was a lot of traffic on the river. I lost count of how many sampans we stopped and boarded but it was a bunch. Once the sun began to set, the traffic began to dwindle.

"I assume everyone is pretty much done for the day," I said to Quacker.

"Not so much that. The night belongs to the VC. The good gooks don't want to get shot up by accident. The others were VC. Oh, they have all the papers and documents and act all nice, but once the sun sets, seventy-five percent are nothing more than good ol' Charlie waiting to waste our ass. Some will just report our last known position and the direction we were headed so the VC can set up an ambush."

"You're yanking my chain, right?" I said, not sure if he was telling the truth or blowing smoke up the new guy's ass.

"I shit-you-not. You wait and in about an hour, there is a good chance we will make contact with Charlie.

I took a quick look at the sky and was somewhat relieved to see that the moon was nothing more than a sliver.

"So, what's the best course of action?" I asked.

"Hug the shoreline. Follow the 913"

"Which side is best?"

"The one the VC aren't on," he suggested.

"Not funny and definitely and not very useful," I shot back.

"Man, we roll the dice and take our chances," was his reply.

We were slowly moving along the bank on our port side. I had my hand fully planted on the throttles in case I had to hit it to get the boat out of the kill zone. I had also already decided I would feint like I was going to make a 180 degree turn but then jag back and go full ahead hoping they wouldn't have time to react.

I noticed Skeeter and Tex were watching the shoreline intently. They both had their guns trained on the starboard shore. Quacker had the 7.62 x .51 aimed at the port shore. We motored along for a good half hour before the radar picked up a boat moving down the river toward us. I put the boat in idle and we just drifted. The 913 stopped and reversed slightly letting us take the lead. I wasn't exactly sure why they did. Maybe they wanted to see how we handled ourselves.

The boat was just around a sharp bend and moving slowly. Quacker tapped Skeeter on the shoulder and pointed to where the sampan would pop out from behind the bend. No one said a word as we waited. I had the high-powered field glasses trained on the spot. I saw the bow come around first then the rest of the boat. Suddenly it started to turn and head back. I moved the throttles fully forward and within seconds we were baring down on the sampan.

I saw one of the people on board dive into the water and the one steering with the motor was trying to make it to the port bank. Skeeter opened up with the twin .50's and riddled the sampan. I saw one guy go over the side and the boat suddenly stopped and was just floating. Either we had killed everyone or they had all abandoned the sampan.

Tex and Quacker appeared at the side of the boat with their M16's at the ready. I grabbed mine and cut the engines back to idle. We drifted alongside of the boat and everyone had their guns trained on the craft that appeared to be pretty shot up.

"Want me to go aboard?" Tex asked.

"Skeeter, pump a few rounds into it with your M16," I said.

Skeeter opened fire and shot a whole magazine into the boat from bow to stern. No one was alive on that boat. Just as I was about to okay Tex boarding a body floated by face down. The black Bo Doi had two large holes in it. From the size, I guess he was hit with the .50 cal. from Skeeter.

"Yeah, go ahead and check it out," I told Tex and he scampered down on the boat. It almost went to the water line immediately.

"Hey, this thing is leaking like a sieve," he yelled.

"Okay, come on off. We will just sink the damn thing right here," I said.

Tex climbed back on board and I could see his boots were soaking wet along with his pant cuffs. Quacker grabbed a M40 and shot a round into it. The boat blew in half from the explosion. I learned one thing. I needed to back the boat up a little further when using the M40. One end went under but the other was still floating. The hell with wasting more ammo, I shoved the throttles forward and we ran right over the thing. When I looked back it was totally gone. Whatever they had on board didn't make it this time. I hoped it was something valuable that they really needed.

The 913 pulled alongside of us and shouted over, "Well done. Blew those gooks to hell" and gave me a peace sign.

The rest of the night was free of problems. We only got one other blip on the radar but it was pretty far away and I figured by the time we got there they would be long gone. After patrolling for eleven hours we turned the boats around and headed back to the docks.

I made my after-action report, which was getting easier to do, and submitted it to the LT.

The next day was all about maintenance. This is Lake's specialty. He was our go to man for any mechanical problems but I had a pretty good handle on the system. The only thing I didn't know was about the jet drive. I spent the entire day with Skeeter as he went about the maintenance check list. Service to the engine is critical when you are getting ready to potentially go into a firefight.

"Is that everything?" I asked when he said we were done.

"Well, I didn't change out the injectors but it isn't really time yet."

"Let's go ahead and do it. I've never played around with a diesel engine before," I told him.

He kind of rolled his eyes but I let it pass. Maybe he didn't think it was important but I sure the hell did. After we finally finished I went to find Quacker. He was working on the twin 50's up on the bow.

"What ya doing my man?" I asked.

"Just working on the 50's."

"Yeah, I can pretty much see that. What I mean is what is that part you have in your hand?"

"The barrel extension."

"Where are the rest of the parts" I said.

"The barrel is right there; the receiver assembly is still attached. All the rest of the parts are right here," he said holding up an oversized ditty bag.

"You mind if I stick around and watch a while. I need to know how to disassemble and re-assemble one of these things."

"Good thing to know. I'll lay the major groups out and then explain how it all goes together," he explained.

As he set them out he explained what the function of each part was and the nomenclature.

"This is the barrel group. Next is receiver group, then the barrel extension group, bolt group, barrel buffer assembly group, driving spring rod, and the back assembly."

"And all those other parts?" I asked.

He shook his head and said, "Geez, I don't know. Extra parts I guess."

I just looked at him until he laughed.

"Hang on and I'll show you how all of this goes together."

He assembled the weapon and then walked me through taking it back apart. Without his coaching, I would probably still be there trying to figure it all out. He broke it down again and when it was finally apart, he told me to re-assemble it the way he had shown me.

"You want me to do this by myself?"

"Sure, that's the best way to learn. Besides, you can bet I will check it out before we go out again."

Sure enough, he went off to get some chow and I started working on the gun. Sweat was pouring off me by the time I got it all put back together. At least I had no left-over parts.

When he came back he seemed surprised that it was back in combat condition and ready to rock n roll. He checked it over carefully before loading the belt linked .50 cal. rounds.

"When we go out, you get to shoot it first," he said.

"Chicken."

"Damn straight."

Later when we did go out, I fired the .50 and it worked like a charm.

"Beginners luck," Quacker grudgingly admitted.

I honestly think it kind of shocked him that I got it right the first time. I wondered if it was a test of some kind to see how sharp I was. If it was he must have been convinced I was at least sharp enough to captain the boat.

The next week was just routine patrols. Boredom mixed in with an adrenalin rush as you stopped a sampan and tried to watch everyone at the same time. You knew you couldn't let your guard down for even a second or you or your crew could be dead. We only had one sampan try to escape but a burst from the .50's stopped them dead. They had been hauling ammunition. Lots of 7.62 x .39 caliber rounds that were used in the VC Ak-47's.

They were hauled off to wherever the ARVIN's took prisoners. I would imagine it wasn't a very nice place.

CHAPTER EIGHT

Things fell into a routine if you could call it that. Boredom followed by a period of fear when approaching a sampan and inspecting the cargo. Your concentration could never waver for even a moment.

My first month had passed and then another. The one big fire fight and a few small skirmishes. Other than that, things were quiet. We were on the 2400 – 1200 duty patrol and the night had been routine. Traffic was even less than normal.

It was just starting to get light and we motored into a sort of eerie fog that was hanging on the water and the tops of the trees. It was thicker than I had ever seen it before so we were really relying on radar to help us pick our way upriver.

A sampan would suddenly just appear out of the fog just a few feet in front of our boat. We were working with Captain Lance and his crew on the other PBR. We stopped to check out a sampan and they just sort of drifted on by a few yards. I could still see the stern of their boat.

We went about the routine inspection. We had checked their

papers and ID's and were just about to shove them off. Quacker handed out several packs of cigarettes to the people on the boat when a sudden explosion rocked our boat and a large fireball lit up the fog. It came from Lance's boat.

At first, I couldn't understand what happened then I realized that their boat had been hit by something. I shoved the throttles forward and made an arch around to the front of the boat. It was then that I saw they had stopped a large cargo barge and it was trying to pull away.

Quacker, Tex, and Skeeter were already firing on the barge. I could see the tracers ripping into the side and bow. Quacker was aiming just above the waterline working back and forth. I raced our boat around the barge and the men opened up on the other side of the boat. One VC stood up for just a second and aimed an RPG at us but Tex literally cut him in half. His body fell back in the boat and his head and trunk fell in the water.

"Swimming to the shore," Skeeter yelled, pointing to two VC trying to reach the shore. I flipped the boat around and headed straight for them. I didn't even stop; I just ran over the top of them. I reversed the boat direction and idled, waiting for them to surface if they were still alive. We sat there for a full two minutes before I throttled over to Lance's boat.

I could see where the RPB had hit just below the twin .50's tub. The Gunner's Mate, a guy I knew only as 'Rocky' was missing his left arm and most of his head. He was obviously dead.

We pulled alongside and Tex and Skeeter, jumped on board the PBR. Lance was lying on his back with a huge hole in his chest and his right leg was just gone. He was dead by the time they tried to even get a compression bandage on his chest wound. The other two, Pickles, a skinny, red haired kid with freckles by the hundreds was holding his right arm, and Dog, the EM 3, was the only one not hit.

"Lance is dead, isn't he?" Pickles asked.

"Yeah, Rocky as well," Skeeter told them.

"I think my arm is broken," Pickles said.

"Thank goodness it isn't a compound fracture. At least I don't think it is," Tex told him.

"How about you Dog?"

"I'm cool man. Far freakin' out. A piece, one of the barrels, I think, from the .50's rammed right into the engine hatch. Missed my head by an inch."

"From the looks of it, I doubt this thing will run in its present condition. We will tow you back to base. I'm sure Iceman has probably already called it in," Tex told him.

"Iceman?" Dog asked.

"Yeah, after today I'm gonna call Frenchie, Iceman. He reacted and kept us safe while cutting down the barge. Pretty cool for a guy that has been here for only a few months," Tex said.

"Iceman. I like it man," Skeeter agreed.

We threw a line over to the PBR and secured it. Once it was tied off I edged over to the barge and all three of my men went aboard. There was no one there. I waited for what seemed like a lifetime before Tex popped back up on the stern.

"Man, you ain't gonna' believe what we frickin' found on this thing."

"Okay, but will it float? Can we haul it back to the base?" I yelled back.

"Skeeter and Quacker are shoring it up the best they can. It will take a few minutes. You called this in, right?"

"Yeah, sit rep is already in. They are sending a Huey to watch over us while we make our way back. The LT doesn't want us to run into an ambush. They have intel saying there is a build-up near An Hoa," I shouted.

"Okay, we should be done in just a few more minutes," Tex said and disappeared again.

No more than five minutes later my men were back on board along with Dog and Pickles. The stricken PBR was going to be a struggle to pull along with the barge but I felt they both needed to be taken back. I eased the throttles forward and ever so slowly we began to make way. It was going to be a long trip back.

We were about two klicks down river when we heard the slick slicing through the air. A few seconds later it popped into view. It circled us and fell in by doing slow looping rings while we headed home. Everyone was tense and the news from base that a new report had confirmed a build-up of VC in the An Hoa area. It was believed that the Charlies were NVA which caused even greater apprehension. Not so much because they were any tougher to fight but because they had access to more sophisticated weapons.

We were no more than five klicks from An Hoa when two fast movers came streaking in from down river. We watched as they unloaded Napalm bombs on the edge of the river just a few hundred yards from where we were.

You could feel the percussion and heat as they exploded leaving the familiar black plumb of smoke and the accustomed smell that only Napalm has. We could hear secondary explosions so we knew they had hit their target.

We cleared the area and not a single shot was fired in our direction. The rest of the trip was anticlimactic. I beached my craft to make it easier for the barge and damaged PBR to be pulled ashore.

The LT was waiting for us along with almost everyone else. Everyone looked down in the mouth. The word about Lance and Rocky had already made the rounds.

I walked up to the LT and gave him a run down on what had happened. Tex and Skeeter were helping Pickles out of the boat.

"The bodies are pretty badly damaged."

"I gathered. Would you mind if your men put them in the bags? I don't think it would do anyone good to see the condition they are in," he asked.

"No problem. I agree that would be best. We didn't find all the body parts."

"Just do what you can," he replied.

"You want me to leave them on the boat?"

"No. I'll have a truck backed down to your boat and you can load them on to that."

"Got it."

"What's on the barge?" he asked as if seeing it for the first time.

"I haven't seen it yet but my guys tell me it is a hell of a find."

"I'm gonna' check it out. Want to join me?"

"Wouldn't miss it for the world," I said as we climbed on board the barge.

We both stopped and looked at each other when we saw what we had captured. Lance had captured this at the cost of his life. There were twenty crates of RPG's, boxes and thirty boxes of mortar rounds, at least a hundred crates of ammunition. On top of that we found fifty anti-personnel mines, ten SA-7 Russian surface to air missiles and one hundred-fifty AK-47's.

While all of that was impressive, perhaps the most mystifying thing of all was two full American pilots' uniforms, complete with helmets. Patches on the uniform indicated they were from the 834 Air Force Division stationed at Tan Son Nhut Air Base, just outside of Saigon.

"What do you think they were going to try to do, steal an Air Force plane?" I asked.

"You never know. Lots of C-130 there including 'Puff'."

"The new C-130 gunship?"

"That's the one," the LT replied.

"Yikes. If they could steal that the Army would be up a creek with no paddle."

"So, would we," he said shaking his head.

"What about IV Corps? Don't they need to be notified?"

"I'll take care of that. You and your guys start getting the bodies off the PBR.

It was the last thing I wanted to do but I knew that it had to be done. I got my crew together, we gathered the body bags and headed for Lance's destroyed PBR.

It was my first real look at the carnage. There was blood, body parts, and Rocky's brains were splattered all over the tub where he had been firing the 50.'s. It was also my first look up close at a real dead person other than at a funeral. This was nothing like that. It took some effort not to barf as we finally got his body out of the tub and pulled him up on the main deck where we placed him in a body bag.

Lance was no better, the only difference being that he was already on deck and all we had to do was get him in the bag. It was weird picking up his leg and putting it in with him but I didn't know what else to do with it.

I took one of the dog tags off each of the men's chain and put them in my pocket to give to the LT. By the time we were all done and the bags zipped up, the truck had arrived and we struggled to get the bodies to shore and loaded.

It was the first time I had stopped and looked at my uniform. It was blood stained from my chest to my knees. My men had fared no better.

When we were done I went to the
CP and handed the dog tags over to
the LT and then went and took a
shower and changed uniforms.

CHAPTER NINE

That night, lying on my cot, I had time to reflect on what had happened. I mean, one minute everything was routine and then suddenly all hell had broken lose. Two men had died in the blink of an eye. I seriously doubt that either man knew exactly what happened.

Lance had been in country for nine months and was totally focused and yet it didn't really matter. Rocky had forty-five and a wake-up before he went back to the real world. I heard he was getting married to his high school sweetheart as soon as he returned.

I also realized that up until now, I thought I was invincible but this...this thing just happened. Could I have done anything different if it had been our boat that had taken the lead? Lance was a sharp guy, well-seasoned and Rocky was considered to be one of the best gunners in our group and in the end, what difference did it make?

Just before I drifted off to sleep, I realized I had never even given a thought to the VC I had run over. I had just reacted at seeing the enemy in the water. I wasn't sure what to make of that but one thing for sure, it didn't bother me to hit them.

I had come pretty far in just a few months and it made me wonder what I would be like when my tour was over. I had never even hunted before and now I was killing people.

The next morning everyone was up but a dark cloud was hanging over everyone's head. Pickles had been sent to the field hospital to have his arm looked at. Dog was sitting alone eating I and I went over and sat beside him.

"How you doing?"

"Doing? I feel like shit."

"Yeah, I'm with that. Any idea what happens next?"

"Frickin' Nam," he shouted at no one in particular.

"Got it man. Want to talk about it?"

"What's to talk about? Lance is dead, Rocky is dead, and Pickles is in the hospital and here I sit without a damn scratch on me," he agonized.

"How would it have helped if you were wounded or killed? Would that make it any better?' I asked him.

"Man, you are missing the point. I didn't get a damn hangnail even. That makes me feel like crap," he said, putting his head down on the table.

"Look Dog, it just wasn't your time. You know that. It could have been you we pulled out of the boat, instead of one of the others. It's all just a crap shoot. Either you get your ass shot off or you get away to fight again another day," I said.

I am not a philosopher so I was just pulling this out of my butt. I was trying to find something to say that would make him at least understand that he didn't do anything wrong. The wheel of life and death just didn't happen to land on his number. I really wanted to come up with something brilliant to say but honestly, I just couldn't think of anything. He finished his meal, such as it was, and got up and drifted off without another word.

As I was leaving the LT came up and said he had a mission to talk to me about. We headed over to the CP and he had me take a seat.

"I want you and your crew to go on a special mission. I'll be brutally frank; it has a high-risk factor."

"Whatever you need LT"

"Better listen to what I have to say before you decide. This is going to be a single boat mission. You are going to pick up a LRRP patrol just a few klicks upriver. No one knows they are even there. You are to take them to this area," he said pointing to a large map of the entire Delta Region.

"Whoa. We can't make it that far of a tank of fuel."

"Yes, you can. You will have extra fuel on board and we have set up a refueling stop at this point," he said, pointing to the map again.

"Isn't Neak Loeang in Cambodia? It sure looks like it to me," I asked.

"Yes, it is."

"And we are authorized to enter Cambodian space?"

"The orders come from IV Corps and have been approved by President Johnson."

"Alright LT, give me all the details," I asked.

"You will leave here at zero dark thirty. Five klicks upriver you will be guided to the where the LRRP's are holed up. Once they are on board, you will immediately head upriver. You will have to use one of the barrels of fuel to make it to the resupply point. It is located right here," he said tapping the chart.

"At that point, Peam Chor, you will find extra fuel. The LRRP's have already been told that you are totally in charge until they reach their destination. They are to act as deck hands when refueling."

"Good luck with that," I replied.

"They will do as told. After you refuel, you will spend the night there, hidden as best as possible out of sight. You will not leave until 0100 hours. That will put them on station at the exact time they need to be situated and minimize the possibility of discovery. As soon as they are off the boat, you head immediately back to the refueling station. Top off your tanks and wait until they contact you for extraction."

"Wait? You mean we just hide out until they are ready to get out of Dodge?"

"Exactly. Once they contact you, you go back and extract them and get back to base. If all goes well, Cambodia will never even know we were there."

"If all goes well. That is a huge if," I said.

"Yes, it is, but this is a critical mission," the LT said.

"Aren't they all?"

"Consider this one more criticaler, if there is such a word."

"Alright. I'll update my maps and plan out the route. There are a bunch of islands on the way upriver," I told him.

"Hopefully, no one is on them when you go by at that time of night. I would like to see your final plan," he said and I was dismissed.

I headed back to the boat and gathered the crew around. I gave them all the skinny I had on the operation. A lot of mumbling but no real moaning and groaning. They were good men and would do what was asked of them.

"How many LRRP's?" Tex asked.

"Three."

"We are going to need extra rations," Skeeter pointed out.

"Been taken care of," I told him.

"Well the LRRP's aren't getting any of mine," Tex chimed in.

"You guys know what to do. Make sure we have enough water and ammo. I honestly don't have any idea what we will get into," I told them

"Iceman, did you volunteer us for this mission?"

"I may be dumb but I'm not stupid. We were volunteered."

"Okay, I'm cool with that," Quacker replied.

The boat was ship-shape and all provisions stowed by noon so I had the men knock off and sack out. That is easier said than done. The heat, humidity, and bugs are a constant enemy, along with the damn rats and mosquitos that I swear could take a round from an M-16 and keep on going.

It got slightly cooler once the sun set but the humidity didn't seem to change all that much. There was no wind to speak of so you just sort of cooked in your own juices.

At 2200 hours I went to see the LT to get any last-minute instructions. The mission was a 'go' so I checked my charts against the posted ones to make sure they were up to date. Areas of possible enemy incursion were marked and I copied them onto my map as well.

Finished with the briefing I headed to the boat and did my usual check. The extra fuel was lashed on board and extra C-rats were stored in every nook and cranny. Tex always had this fear of running out of food.

The LT came down to the boat and wished us luck. I was surprised to see Dog standing with him.

"You got room for an extra hand?" the LT asked.

What was I going to say? He knew the situation as well as anyone. The boat was already going to be loaded down pretty much but I knew what he was trying to do. He wanted to get Dog up and back in the saddle as quickly as possible.

"What do you think Dog?" I asked him.

"Yeah. I would like to come along if you can use me," he replied.

"You have a lot of experience. We can always use another set of eyes and hands. Hop aboard and we will get this show on the road," I told him.

The LT nodded his appreciation before turning and heading back to the CP. It was time to get going. I looked at my watch and it was coming up on 0030 hours. I fired up the engines, let them idle a few seconds then slowly pulled away from the dock.

As we went by the bank I saw Dog look over at a torn up PBR like the one we were on presently. I gunned the throttles, there was no time to think about that now.

CHAPTER TEN

We slowly cruised up the river looking for the spot the LRRP's were sitting in waiting. Quacker pointed to a red light that blinked four times. That was our indication of where to pull in. I eased the boat onto the shore and within seconds the three LRRP's were on board.

"Lieutenant Collins," he said shaking my hand, "This is Reynolds and Taylor, my other team members."

"Nice to meet you. MM1 Martin. My crew," I said pointing out each man. Quacker on the 50.'s, Tex on the back .50, Skeeter our EM and Dog will be taking up one of the M60's when we get closer to our fuel depot."

"Anything we can do to help?"

"Just relax for now. Grab some shuteye if you can. We have a long way to go. When we need fuel, we will need your help."

"Not a problem. Just tell us what you need," the Lieutenant replied.

"Will do," I replied.

While it was nerve racking, we had patrolled these waters before and in this area the only threat had come from sampans that wouldn't stop. Even those we always had the upper hand except for the one-time Lance's PBR got blown out of the water.

Once we cleared our normal patrol area the tension ratcheted up another notch. My guys were constantly scanning the shore on both sides of the river. When we came to a split in the river we all knew the probability of an ambush increased. The river would narrow making maneuvering even more difficult.

All along the cost we could hear raging battles taking place off in the distance. We all watched fascinated as Puff lit up the sky with a stream of red tracers. It was an amazing sight that none of us would ever forget. The only thing I knew for sure was that I sure would hate to be on the receiving end.

Mile by mile we traveled up the river, waiting for something to happen but even in a situation like this, adrenalin can only carry you so far. Obviously the LRRP's were used to it because they were racked out, not worrying about a thing. The thought to have Quacker open up on the .50's crossed my mind, but I realized that wouldn't be very smart. Someone was bound to start looking for the source.

Instead we just continued to head deeper and deeper into the Vietnam interior. I had been studying my charts to try to get an accurate fix on our location. The fuel depot was critical for our being able to complete the mission. If I missed it, we would be up the creek without a paddle. Literally.

I called Dog and Skeeter over and had them look at the charts.

"I think we are right about here," I said pointing to the map.

They both grabbed binoculars and started scanning the horizon.

"Man, I don't know. That island looks like a hundred others," Skeeter said.

"I think we will know better when we get past this island. We should be able to see this protrusion right across from Peam Chor. If that's the case, we aren't too far from the fuel depot," Dog replied.

Just then the engines sputtered. I had been watching the gauges and knew it was time to refuel. I didn't want them to go dry because diesels engines are hard to start once air gets in the line. I shut them down immediately and we were enveloped by total silence.

The LRRP's reacted immediately, grabbing their weapons, and standing up.

"Easy guys. Just getting ready to refuel. We are coming up on Peam Chor and then it won't be long to the fuel at Leuk Daek," I whispered to them.

"Need our help?"

"I'm sure the guys could use a hand with the 55-gallon barrel," I told the Lieutenant.

In less than ten minutes the barrel was emptied into the boat's tank and I restarted the engines. Thirty seconds later we were on our way. The island wasn't all that long and Dog said, "I think you're right. That looks like the area on the map. That," he said pointing, "is Peam Chor by my estimation."

"I agree. We are right where we are supposed to be. It won't be but another forty-five minutes and we should hit Leuk Daek. Of course, finding the depot might be a tad difficult," I replied.

I told the Lieutenant that the minute we found the depot, we need to get the extra fuel onboard as fast as possible and I would need his men's help. We would also off load the empty 55-gallon drum to make more room.

We crept forward watching the shoreline. It was starting to get light which was both a blessing and a curse. We would be more visible in the lighter conditions but on the other hand, it could help us find the fuel.

"Okay, it should be on the port side. See the tip of that island? It is supposed to be directly across from it. It will be back off the bank but visible if we look hard enough," I told everyone.

I edged the boat over as close to the shore as I could get and just idled along.

"There," Dog said, pointing to a row of 55-gallon drums.

"Good eye," I replied and swung the boat so we could nose in.

Everyone was off the boat in seconds except for Tex who I wanted to stay put on the stern .50 just in case. It was no easy task getting the barrels out to the boat and loaded on board. By the time we got the last one up and in place the sun was starting to just peek over the treetops.

No more than a hundred yards further was a small inlet. I nudged the boat in and shut off the engines.

Everyone immediately went about cutting limbs and branches to cover the boat. It would provide cover and keep the sun off us as we spent the day hunkered down.

A few minutes after we felt camouflaged enough, sampans started appearing on the water almost immediately after we finished. If we had been a few minutes later we would have been discovered. We were officially in Cambodia and if we were caught it could cause a hell of a problem for IV Corps not to mention the President. Of course, it would never reach that far. He would disavow all knowledge of such a rogue action.

While we were lollygagging, killing time by playing cards and sleeping, we heard a loud thump that rattled the leaves. It was followed by a huge explosion. This went on for perhaps fifteen minutes. You could see ripples on the water from the detonations.

"Rolling Thunder," Lieutenant Collins said, "B-52's bombing the Ho-Chi-Minh trail. It cuts through Cambodia and south to Vietnam."

"So, we are actively at war with Cambodia as well?" I asked.

"Nah, it's all unofficial. We aren't attacking Cambodia, just the trail," he laughed.

"Seems like a pretty thin line," I replied.

"Yeah, you sure don't want to be on the wrong side of the line when the bombs fall."

Once they were gone we all went back to killing time. Vietnam, I was learning, was more than boredom mixed in with times of unbelievable terror. I was beginning to see how it would grate on your nerves. Some guys let it roll off their backs while others fret over every little sound or assignment.

Traffic started to lessen as the sun began to set. I was anxious to get going. I felt like at any minute someone would discover our location and we would end up in a fire fight, possibly endangering the entire mission.

Finally, the last few stragglers began to head home and it was starting to get dark. I was just about ready to have then uncover the boat when I heard a deep rumble. It sounded like it was coming upriver. Everyone took up defense positions as much as possible. I had backed in so the twin .50's were facing out. Quacker, loaded the chamber and released the safety. Everyone else was ready to cut lose if needed.

Slowly a patrol boat, much like a PBR but bigger came down the river. The bad news was it had a 3" gun on the bow and we were no match for something with that kind of fire power. Our only options would be to outrun it if possible and keep them from lining up a shot.

I'm sure everyone was holding their breath. I know I was. Suddenly a bright light pierced the darkness, bouncing around the island across from us and playing over the water. It was either looking for something or just checking out the area. It swept over our way and I turned my head as the light played over our boat. It kept on going so either they didn't see us or they were trying to lure us out into the open.

After a few minutes, it picked up the pace and finally disappeared into the night. We all let out a sigh of relief. I was glad I had held off on removing our cover. Pure luck.

I wondered if the boat would come back up stream after it finished its rounds. There was nothing I could do about it so I decided not to worry. We would deal with it when the time came.

At last it was 0100 hours and we eased out of the overhang and headed north. The trip wouldn't take more than 90 minutes if everything went well. I kept a close eye on the radar in case the Cambodian boat popped up on our six.

"Over there," the Lieutenant said, pointing to the port side.

"You sure?" I asked.

"I've studied every inch of that area the last three weeks. That's the place," he assured me.

I swung the boat over to the port shore and let it drift up on the bank.

"Good luck," I said, as they climbed off the boat.

"Just be here when we send for you. You have the frequency and password. We will call 90 minutes before extraction," Collins replied.

"We'll be here," I assured him and slowly backed off the bank.

By the time I turned around, they had disappeared into the jungle. Man, just the three of them, in a country that would love to get its hands on Americans. I doubt they would ever be heard from again if they got caught.

We eased on back to the same location and I backed the boat back in the same overhang area. We went about camouflaging the boat but I noticed the crew put a little more effort into it this time. I guess the Cambodian patrol boat sort of shook them up just a little.

CHAPTER ELEVEN

We spent two long days and nights waiting for the extraction order. Have you ever spent 48-hours just sitting around except to go to the head, which was the bushes just to the side of the boat? It was hot, humid and between the flies and mosquitoes, you felt like facing the Cambodian patrol boat would be a better option. Not really, but there is only so much sleep, cards, and eating that can be done during that time.

Tex was writing a long letter to his girl and Dog, Quacker, and Skeeter were playing cards. I swear it sounded like 'go fish', but I wasn't about to ask. With this much time on your hands you can do some deep thinking.

I was wondering what my real motivation for volunteering for Vietnam was. Was I just crazy, hoping to be a hero of some kind, or looking for adventure? Most likely it was a combination of the three with a little desire to see if I could really take it. The manly thing to do? To go against the grain of all the anti-war protesters? To show I was a patriot?

After thinking about for a long while, I finally drifted off to sleep with the constant noise of fighting all around our base. The last thing I remembered thinking before drifted off, that it was probably a combination of all those things. I had always believed in my country and this seemed like a good way to show it. Of course, it could just as easily because I am dumber than a stump and have a death wish. Whatever the reason, it was too late to back out now.

On the third day, we got the call to extract the LRRP's team. We waited until the sun was setting before heading out. I knew it would take about ninety minutes to get to them so I had Tex relay our ETA and set off. It was a cloudless night with a crescent moon so I felt fairly good about making it to the extraction point without much trouble.

Ninety-four minutes later we drifted onto the shore and the LRRP's scrambled on board.

"We need to get a move on. This area is crawling with gooks. A patrol boat came by about an hour ago. We were afraid you might run into them,"

"Didn't see a thing," I said and backed off the bank.

I did a quick 180 degrees and headed down river. We would stop at

Peam Chor and fill up with the last of the fuel and then cruise on home.

I should have known it wouldn't be that simple.

We were only fifteen minutes from Peam Chor when Tex shouted, "RPG."

I looked back and sure enough there it was heading right for us. I had already started turning the boat hard to starboard and doing a quick 180-degree turn. The damn thing hit just behind the stern, sending up a huge stray of water. I looked up and saw a second one streaking for us. I turned hard to port and watched as it grew larger by the second. It went right over the stern and landed twenty yards away. I reversed directions until we were heading down stream once again. Water splashed up just in front of us, no more than ten feet from the bow. Two more landed close and I started zigzagging back and forth as much as the river would allow.

They were firing 82mm mortars at us and from the rate that they were hitting, there had to be more than one. A minute later we were out of range but we had blown right by our fuel depot. No way was I going back, besides, I figured they had already found it and hauled it off.

I throttled back to conserve fuel and decided there wasn't anything further I could do. Twenty minutes later we cleared Cambodia's territory and that made me feel a little better. Not a lot, but at least we were back in Nam.

Reflecting on the situation it reminded me of how crazy war is. We were all bored out of our minds waiting for the LRRP's to finish up so we could head back. Then all of a sudden, you are fighting for your life and the adrenalin rush is unbelievable. The thing is, I don't remember many of the details, I was too busy doing what I was trained to do. I didn't even give a thought to getting hit or the boat blown out of the water. I looked down and the floor was littered with spent cartages but honestly, that part hardly registered on me. It makes sense everyone would be shooting but at the time it was just background noise that I was hardly aware of.

Around three a.m. I heard the engines sputter. I saw Skeeter immediately jump up. I looked over at the fuel gauges and knew we were in a world of hurt. We were still four hours from base with diesel fuel. Without fuel, it would take several more hours by drifting. We would also be sitting ducks for any VC in the area. I called in a sit rep and informed them of our problem.

They woke the LT and he came on the horn and said that they would send out two boats with extra fuel. Just to float on down and they would meet up with us. What choice did we have? The only thing I was concerned about was another ambush. Time takes forever when you are waiting. One hour seemed like three. Everyone, including the LRRP's were tense. Finally, when it was going on five A.M., I heard the throaty roar of our PBR's heading up stream. They rounded a corner and we all let out a sigh of relief. Thirty minutes later we were fueled and heady to go.

Once I parked the boat the LRRP's shook all our hands and disappeared into the early morning mist. LT Ellis came down to the boat and congratulated us on a job well done. He wanted a full report so I headed to the hooch and started writing. I was getting much better at filling out the required action reports. Half of it is learning the correct jargon so someone higher up doesn't go ape shit.

When I was finished, I took it to the LT and he read through it. He only made two changes and then asked me to sit down. Usually I just dropped them off, he would peruse them and I would be on my way. I took a seat on one of the crates and waited.

"I'm sending Bonner and Keller down. Bonner because he has pretty much lost his nerve. He is afraid of everything and it is affecting his crew's moral. Two of them came to talk to me about it. Keller only has a week to go before he hits the real world. I can't see making him go out on another mission. That leaves Nelson as the senior man and he only has a few weeks left. You need to get ready to take on the responsibility of senior enlisted man," he said.

"Whoa. LT, I've only been here a few months. I'm not sure I'm ready for that kind of responsibility,"

"Well, that's why I'm telling you now. You have three weeks to get ready. That's just the way it is. Look, I've already seen how you have fit in. Your crew has a lot of good things to say about you. You know they have named you 'Iceman', because you are cool under fire," he said.

"I may look cool but my guts are churning on the inside," I replied.

"That may be true, but you maintain your composure, so they are better able to do their jobs. It's the same for all real leaders. Never let them see you sweat. If you panic, they all panic and that leads to people getting killed in war."

"Yes sir. I'll give it my best shot."

"I know you will. Don't hesitate to come to me if you feel frustrated. Nothing wrong with getting advice from time to time."

"Thank you, LT, I appreciate that," I replied.

When I got back to the boat everyone had taken off for chow. I was glad because I needed time to think what this would mean. I don't lack confidence and I am not overly worried about myself but now I would be the one sending the crews out.

***

The next few weeks were routine. Twelve hours out every other day but by staying close to base the chance of a firefight was minimal. Bonner was sent to Saigon for evaluation but I spent the afternoon with him when we had some down time. It wasn't exactly his nerves. It was more like realizing how crazy this war was. We would patrol up and down the river and the thousands of tributaries and to what end?

We could have a firefight and kick the hell out of the VC but a week later they were right back at it and we would do it all again. It wasn't like we were making any real progress. Sure, we killed a bunch of little men running around in their black PJ's but what did we really get out of it?

In WW II you captured land and held it. In Nam, you fought a battle and it didn't really change a thing, except for people on both sides getting killed. Didn't anyone really have a plan for how this would all end? I can only tell you this, from the common fighting man's perspective, it was a real FUBAR. I doubt if one person in all South Vietnam had any idea what the hell was going on in the boonies. They were all sitting on their fat asses eating hot chow and drinking. Put them out here for a few months and see if that didn't change the way this war was being fought.

The LT came by with some bad news. Poor Keller. His chopper was hit by an RPG just a few klicks from here. It went down close to a VC base and a rescue mission found the gunship but only the pilot and co-pilot were inside.

Either he was able to somehow escape or was now a POW. The location was just a few hundred yards from one of the tributaries.

We talked it over as a group and all agreed we wanted to go and search the area in case he had managed to escape. We knew he would head for the water thinking we would most likely look for him there. Of course, that assumed he wasn't now in the hands of the gooks.

The other boat captains and I went to talk to the LT about a rescue mission.

"Look guys, the chance of actually finding Keller is slim to none. We don't even know if he was able to get out of the area," he reasoned.

"LT please. Keller has survived for his whole tour. He knows what it's like and his boat was taken out once before and he managed to survive. It is the least we can do," I argued.

"You don't even know where to start looking," the LT said.

"Yeah, look," I replied, laying a map on the table, "This is where the chopper went down according to the reports. It's less than a mile to the water. I'm sure he will head in that direction if he didn't get taken. It's what I would do. We're sailors, we are most at home in the water. I figure four boats would work best. Two to sneak ashore and head out looking for him and two to motor up and down the search area in case he is waiting along the bank."

"Guys, you don't even know how badly he is hurt. He may not have been able to get to the water for all you know."

"Sir, we have to try. I sure the hell don't want to leave him to the gooks," I said.

He looked at each of us for a few seconds and said, "This has to be a voluntary mission. No one is forced to take this on."

"We all understand that."

"How many are willing to go?'

All eight captains raised their hands."

"I see. Alright French, this is your party. You make the selections. Report back when you are ready to go," the LT said.

"We're ready to go right now. The four boats are loaded and I've picked

Conway, Willis, and Parker to go with me."

"I guess you were pretty sure I would give in," he replied.

"No sir, but we know what kind of a man you are and the last thing you want to do is leave someone behind."

"Alright you knuckle heads, get out of here and bring Keller back if possible."

"Thank you, sir," I said and we all saluted him.

"Go," he said pointing to the tent door.

CHAPTER TWELVE

The area the chopper went down in was near Hiêp Dúc. The only problem, as they say; is you can't get there from here. It wasn't all that far as the crow flies. Unfortunately, we weren't crows. We were going to have to head west to go east. We left Vĩnh Long at zero-dark thirty, heading towards Ton Ngāi. We turned north once we cleared tin Ngāi and wound our way back east towards Hiêp Dúc.

I glanced at my watch and felt pretty good about our progress. We were reaching the point that would take us up the channel to where the chopper went down.

I called over to the other captains and told them to space out a little further. I didn't want us all bunched up. Once we reached the small tributary heading towards the downed craft, I had Parker and Willis go on ahead of us and we hung back. Our boats would beach and our crews would go ashore. I decided to leave Flower, sorry, Cracker on the boat to man the 50's.

When we got within a few hundred yards of where the chopper reportedly went down, I had Conway nose his boat on shore and I did the same. As much as I wanted to shut down the engines, I decided that if something happened and they didn't fire up immediately for some reason, we would be in a world of hurt. I was willing to risk the sound of the idling engines, hoping the dense forest would deaden the sound.

"Just don't shoot us," I said to Cracker and we climbed off the boat.

The two crews formed up, staying a few yards apart and we headed into the jungle. I took point which was probably a stupid thing to do but none of us were infantry men so it didn't seem fair to let someone take that chance. My biggest fear was not recognizing a booby trap and getting us blown to hell and back. I took it very slowly and I'm sure a real grunt would just laugh at my caution.

We were maybe eight or nine hundred yards into the vegetation and I noticed it suddenly seemed very quiet. Not just quiet but a total lack of noise. I had everyone take a knee and I slowly crept forward. When I pulled back a branch I could see a patrol of VC walking almost parallel to us. I counted six and was kind of surprised that two of them were talking and laughing. I kept waiting for them to react the low murmur of the PBR's engines. Fortunately, they were too busy talking to notice.

I gave a brief thought to opening up on them but decided we needed a lot more information. They could well be just part of a much larger force. Conway saddled up by me and I whispered about the VC. He seemed anxious to take them on but I wasn't convinced it was a good idea.

I waited until they were down the trail and then we switched over to the trail they had been on. I figured it wouldn't be booby trapped if they had just ditty-bopped down it.

I smelled smoke and we all immediately got off the trail. I crept ahead and sure enough, I could see a VC camp that looked to have at least fifty solders cooking and generally lollygagging around. A few were cleaning their weapons which surprised me because I though AK's never needed cleaning.

I was getting a very uneasy feeling that we were close to stirring up a hornet's nest. We edged back deeper into the forest and started skirting the area.

Two hundred yards later a hand reached out from the bushes and grabbed my ankle. I almost let out a yell but somehow managed to hold it in. Keller was looking up at me smiling.

"Damn, you guys are a sight for sore eyes," he said standing and throwing his arms around me.

"You didn't really think we were just going to leave you out here did you?"

"Man, I can't believe you are really here."

We all took a knee and I posted two guards to keep a watch on things while I assessed Keller. He had two black eyes and a deep cut on his right cheek.

"Can you walk?" I asked.

"I have a sprained ankle but I can hobble along. I can do whatever I need to do to get out of the place."

"The boat is back that away," I said pointing, "Maybe a half a mile or so. Can you make it or do we need to carry you?"

"I'll make it," Keller replied.

"We need to go slowly. The gooks have patrols out and I don't know shit about tripwires for bobby traps," I told him.

I gave him some C-rats and let him eat before we started back. He was weaker than he thought. Right now, he was going on adrenalin but that would wear off soon once we started humping it back to the boat.

I was dead on. Twenty minutes later we had to stop and let him rest. We had to do that twice more as his energy was nearing depletion. I figured one more good push and we would reach the river. I could smell the water so I knew we were close.

Just as we stood up, Ak's opened up on our position. We all hit the ground and tried to determine where they were coming from. We all opened fire in the general direction they sounded like they were shooting from. I knew we couldn't have a sustained firefight. First, we didn't have all that much ammo. Second, they knew exactly where we were but we were guessing at where they were. Most importantly, they had a lot more troops they could send for and we were in no position to hold them off.

"Fall back and stay low. We need to get to the boat," I yelled.

We scrambled as fast as we could while bullets flew all around us. I was amazed that no one was hit. Conway and I stayed behind and laid down covering fire while the others practically drug Keller along.

We both emptied our magazines on our M16's and started firing our Colt 1911's and then ran like hell. Conway suddenly dropped to the ground and I stopped to see if he was hit. He had just tripped over a root so I grabbed him up by his shirt and we beat feet. We could hear them crashing through the forest behind us and we were both damn happy when we saw the PBR's sitting there. Both boats opened up on the area just behind us and within minutes they stopped firing.

We didn't waste a second and hopped on the boats. Keller was already sitting against the cabin when I floored the throttles. We joined the other boats and headed full speed back to base. I called in and let the LT we had found Keller and that he was in good shape all things considered.

I could tell by his voice he was surprised that we had been successful but was pleased. When we got back to the base everyone was there to greet us. Man, saving another sailor is the greatest feeling in the world. The LT was so caught up he hugged Keller and all the captains.

"I want to see you in the CP. I want to hear all about this before you write up the after-action report," he told me.

That was definitely a new wrinkle. I followed him back to the CP but he said little until we got inside.

"I have to tell you; I gave that mission about as much as a snowball's chance in hell. I never thought you would find him and even if you did I figured he was a goner for sure."

"We got lucky. We did run into a couple of patrols of VC and they do have a base camp in that area. I think we should have a couple of slicks go in there and kick some serious ass," I said.

"Sounds like a plan. Hang on," he said and raised the two choppers that were available to us. "Boys, we have a chance to kill some gooks, you up for it? Good, come on down to the CP and talk to the boat captain that can locate them for you."

When he finished talking, he laid the large map on the table and had me show him where we beached and where the camp was located. It wasn't quite as easy as I thought but I eventually was able to locate the vicinity.

By the time the flyboys arrived I was confident I knew where their base was located. I went over the incident with them and pointed out where I thought I had seen them.

"Hey, let's roll. You want to come with us?" he asked.

"Hell yes," I answered and then looked at the LT.

"Go on, you deserve a little fun."

I ran and got my M16, ammo, and helmet and headed for the slicks. The pilot, Wildman, introduced me to his co-pilot Roughrider, and the two door gunners, Spike and The Kid.

"What's your name," Spike asked.

"Iceman."

"No shit? Iceman. I like it. Has a nice ring to it. Cool, Iceman," he said.

I'm thinking, 'whatever', but I didn't say anything. I mean, I didn't pick it, the crew did. The engines wound up and the rotors started turning. Soon a cloud of dust was being kicked up and then we were airborne. I think the pilot was showing off a little. He rolled it over and increased the lift vector causing my stomach to want to stay on the ground. I acted cool, like I did this all the time. I saw him peek over his right shoulder but I was in the zone to be the Iceman.

It was easy to guide them back to the location even though it looked totally different from the air. Suddenly, 'The Kid' starting blasting away and I'll be damned if I could see what he was shooting at. Just clearing the guns, I guessed but didn't want to ask.

About a mile out I pointed to the area I thought I had seen them and Widman dropped down to just above the trees. Hell, I thought he was going to clip a few. The guy was fearless. He raised up a little then dove right back down. You could see the VC all running for cover. A few had stopped to shoot at us and everyone on the chopper started raking the area. I was firing my M16 at anything that moved. I doubt I was very affective but what the hell, it was a blast.

The .30 casings were littering the floor and rolling all around the deck of the chopper. Both slicks were firing their rocket launchers, obliterating the area. I could see at least twenty-five bodies on the ground. One VC had grabbed an RPG but before he could even get it to his shoulder, Spike cut him almost in half.

After the last pass, we headed home with everyone high on the after-battle adrenalin rush.

"Far out," The Kid kept saying over and over.

"Way cool," added Spike.

"That was just too far out," The Kid repeated for about the tenth time.

One thing it did teach me is that the slicks have a much better visual aspect and a hell of a lot more fire power. I decided I wouldn't hesitate to call them in if I found my crews in a tight situation.

When we finally got back my crew wanted to know all about it. I tried to keep it somewhat factual but I'm sure a little prevarication slipped in from time to time.

CHAPTER THIRTEEN

It was back to routine patrols for the next couple of months and we were all getting a little complacent, not to mention bored. It was tense when we were searching boats but other than that it was pretty laid back.

As we were returning from a patrol the LT sent for me.

"LT, what's up?"

"Your boat is overdue for an overhaul. I am sending you to the Whitfield County, LST 1169. It's anchored in the Bién Vûng Tau region for a few weeks. I want you and Conway to head out at first light."

"What about the crews?" I asked.

"They go as well. It will give them a much-needed chance at some R&R. Maybe you can hitch a ride to Saigon. Just don't get in big trouble. Use your heads. You will need clean uniforms or you will get busted for sure. Oh, and don't forget to salute the brass. They have nothing better to do than harass soldiers. It makes them think they are really in the war," he said.

"Thanks skipper. The guys will really appreciate this," I told him.

"And shine your shoes. You have to look the part even if it is phony," he said, "I will have a repair authorization form ready when you are ready to leave."

I broke it to the two crews and they were thrilled. As you would expect, the ones remaining behind were less enthusiastic. I tried to assure them that they would get their chance once we got our boats repaired and the engines rebuilt. Boat Captain Parker started to argue about who needed repairs more but I refused to get drawn into his gripe session. I just told him to go see the LT and see if you can get him to change his mind. That ended the argument.

The LT was laid back and took good care of us but he wouldn't tolerate anyone calling his orders into question once he had made a decision. He would listen to suggestions, but when he made up his mind, that was it. I respected him for that.

I dug out my dress whites and was dismayed to see that they looked like crap. There were no bases around where we were, so we didn't have the luxury of having someone do our laundry. One thing for sure, we were all pretty much in the same boat. My neck scarf was creased but that could be overcome. I could shine my shoes with no problem but the pants and top were more gray than white. I found mildew in several places.

As we were getting ready to get underway the next morning the Lieutenant met us at the boat. He handed me the repair form and told us not to worry, the Whitfield had a laundry and would take care of our uniforms.

We departed a little after 0600 hours and headed down river. On the map, it didn't look all that far but once we started off I realized just how far we had to go. I was a little concerned about fuel. When we got to the mouth of the river I knew the ship was moored to the south of us. I headed that way and twenty minutes later I saw it anchored just off Biên Vũng Tàu. There were at least ten or twelve boats tied up alongside of her. I was hoping they weren't all there for repairs.

We presented ourselves to the officer of the deck, remembering to salute the flag first then the officer. He was all decked out in spiffy whites and gave us a rather disdainful look. What the hell did he expect, we were really fighting, not having hot chow and a comfy place to lay our head.

"Are all these boats here for repair?" I asked.

"Some for minor stuff, others more in-depth repairs."

He sent us on our way with directions on how to locate quarters that we could rack out in while we were here. The room was pretty big and had two tier bunk beds. I claimed a lower one that was obviously not being used. I unfolded the mattress and made the bed up before lying my gear on it. I needed to find the person in charge of repairs.

After asking several people, I was finally directed to the Officer in charge of Repairs. I knocked on the door and waited.

"Come."

I opened the door and saw a balding man who looked to be in his late forties sitting behind a desk loaded with papers and folders. When he looked up I could see the tension in his face.

"Don't tell me. You want us to do a repair on your boat."

"Yes sir. Actually, two boats."

He moaned and leaned his head back and looked up at the overhead.

"I told them no more until we get some of these repairs in the que done and yet here you are," he sighed.

"Sorry sir, I'm just following orders."

"I know you are. Let me see your repair order."

I handed it to him and he flipped through the two forms, one for my boat and one for Conway's.

"Is that all? Would you like us to install air conditioning for you as well?"

"That would be great," I answered.

He looked at me a second then broke out laughing.

"Okay, we will get your boats fixed. Right now, you're looking at seven to ten days for all repairs to be completed," he told me.

"Darn, and I was in such a rush to get back to being shot at."

"Okay, Machinist Mate French, you can take your dog and pony show on the road someplace else. One of us has work to do."

I thanked him and headed back to the bunk room. I located the galley on the way back and checked what times they served. I was surprised when I was told they were open most of the time since everyone worked rotating shifts. Cool.

The first two days were great. We explored the ship, spent a lot of time in the galley, swapped stories with the other boat crews and played cards. A lot of cards. A couple of guys were able to hop a ride to Saigon and they came back with wild tales about girls wanting to jump their bones every place they went and cheap beer.

Yeah sure, 'buy me a drink sailor, I love you a long time'. Well until your money runs out. I wanted to see Saigon but there was a lot of tension in the city I was told. Tet, the Vietnamese New Year celebration, was only three weeks away.

Finally, Quacker, Dog, and Tex wore me down and talked me into going over to explore the city. I gave in, put on some fresh BDU's and we hopped a ride to Biên Vûng Tâu.

I don't know what I was expecting but it was trashy and run down. Except for Jeeps, I saw maybe two cars. Everything else was a combination of three-wheelers, motor scooters, and bicycles. There were plenty of bars, beggars, and people selling junk. A few of the bars had rude names but some were kind of like you would find in any rundown section of a city in the US.

Our first stop was at the Olympia Bar which was crowded for so early in the day. There were a mixture of locals and military personnel milling around. Of course, there were Boom-Boom girls that immediately wanted you to buy them a drink.

Good ol' Tex, being the youngest, immediately peeled off with the first girl that asked him to get her a drink. I figured his money wouldn't last long. We managed to find a place to sit and I just watched a very strange world go by. Some army guy was making out with one of the bar girls and while I was watching I saw her slip his watch off his wrist without him even noticing. Two Tiger Piss beers ('33') later we headed a little further down the dirty road. We hit a place called the U.S. Star Bar. We stayed for one beer because the bar girls just wouldn't take no for an answer. After a while it got old so we moved on.

Quacker got excited when he saw a place called Fu Ji that offered steam baths. No way was I going to do that. Not because I'm modest but I wasn't about to put my bare ass on a seat that I had no idea when the last time it had been cleaned.

"But guys, we can get a massage and these chicks are totally amazing," Quacker said.

"And I suppose you can get a 'Deluxe' massage for just a little more," I said.

"Ya' never know," he said grinning.

I left them and went into a place called the Sydney Bar. When I went inside I realized I might have made a huge mistake. Everyone looked over at me.

"Eh Mate, you lost?" one of the guys asked.

"Not really. This is Vietnam, right?"

They all looked at each other and them back at me.

"By God, I think you're right."

"Then I'm in the right place if I can get a beer here," I replied.

"Cheeky booger but what the hell, he's a Yank so I guess we can make allowances," the guy at the end of the bar said.

I sat down between two rather large Australians and ordered a beer. The bartender, a young Vietnamese woman who was nice looking, handed me a Fosters Beer.

"What's this?"

"What's this? Mate, you haven't had real beer until you drink one of these," he said reaching over and popping the top.

"This is none of that crap '33' beer or even, no offence intended, the Schlitz and Falstaff rot gut you guys drink."

I took a big swig and was surprised at how smooth it was compared to our beer. Even the Bud we got sporadically couldn't hold a candle to this stuff.

We sat there and traded war stories for a couple of hours. They seemed to be doing just fine but I knew I was getting soused. I'm not a very good drinker in the first place and I'm pretty sure the Fosters was stronger than our beer.

The Aussies seemed the exact same, even though they were chugging them down two to one for me.

"Hey sailor boy, you are looking a little green around the gills. Maybe that's the natural color for sailors but I doubt it. If you are going to puke, do it outside."

I slid off the barstool and tried to stand. The two Aussies next grabbed me under the arms and helped me out the door. I just made before I spewed all over the ground. For some reason, they thought this was funny and called the others out to watch. All I wanted to do was crawl in a hole and die. After a while they lost interest and went back inside to do some more drinking.

I staggered up the street and didn't even know where I was at the moment. I was lucky, Quacker was coming out of the Steam Bath smiling from ear to ear.

"You don't look so good," he said stating the obvious.

"I need to get back to the ship," I moaned.

"Should have come with me. I got the deluxe massage. I feel great," he said

"I'm so happy for you. Just get me to the dock and then go back and round-up the other guys. We need to head back," I said.

"Oh sure, like they are going to listen to me. You just go back and I'll do what I can, but don't expect much," he said leading me down to the dock.

At this point, I didn't really care what they did. I just wanted to get back to the ship and climb in my fart sack. I finally staggered aboard and the OOD just looked at us and waved us on to our quarters. I guess they are pretty used to these kinds of events.

The next day I felt like death warmed over. I managed to rummage around and find a bottle of aspirin and took four of them. After an hour or so I started to feel almost human so I went to check on my boat. I was disheartened to find that it was still third in the que. That meant we would be stuck out here another week at least.

CHAPTER FOURTEEN

I'm pretty sure most guys in the military are the same in one aspect. When you are in the heat of battle or on patrol all you want to do is get out of the situation with everything attached. The strange part is when you are not on the line, within a few days, you get bored and start to crave action.

I was ready to get back to the base and begin patrols again. I guess it's true, we all find something to bitch about. Tex had worn out his welcome in the numerous card games going on. One group accused him of cheating and we almost ended up in a big free for all but cooler heads finally prevailed.

"Did you cheat?" Quacker asked on the way to the galley.

"Hell, no I didn't cheat. I don't need to with those bozos," he answered indignantly.

"You have been kicked out of almost every game on the ship because you win constantly. I mean, it's like you never lose," Quacker insisted.

"So? I'm a good card player. I watch those jerks for their tell and once I figure that out it's like taking candy from a baby," Tex told him.

"Their 'tell'? What the hell is that?"

"The thing that gives them away when they bet. Everyone does something when they are bluffing or when they have a really good hand. I just look for it and then I know what to do," he explained.

"Isn't that cheating?" Quacker pressed.

"Quacker, they are the ones that are making the gestures, I just pick up on them, and no, it's not cheating," Tex said and stomped off to his bunk.

Four days later we were informed that our boat would be ready once we went over it and signed off on the repairs. Dog, Tex, and Skeeter wanted to go into Vung Tau for a last night celebration. I told them that it was fine with me but make sure they were ready to hit the water at no later than 0700. I wanted to get back to base before it got dark.

At 0700 I went down to the boat and talked to the chief who was already aboard warming up the engines. Conway joined us a few minutes later.

"What do you think?" he asked.

I wasn't sure what he meant but I nodded like I understood.

"Pretty smooth sounding. We replaced the port engine with one we had already rebuilt. The starboard engine was in better shape so we just rebuilt it. New cylinder liners, pistons, con rods, and bearings. We re-worked the heads as well. You should have no problem with this baby for a long time."

"Far out," I replied.

"Oh, we checked out the gear boxes and made some minor repairs. The engines have break-in oil in then so take it easy until you get back to your base. Once you get there, make sure your engineman replaces the oil and checks the gear box."

"I'll make sure he does," I told him.

"As you can see you have the latest upgrade to your radar system so you will be able to get a much better picture of what is out there and the range is almost fifty percent more."

"That's awesome," I said.

"I tried to get authorization to put a mini gun on this thing to replace the two 50's, but got shot down. I think it would be so cool to have one of those up front. You could blow anything out of the water with just one pull of the trigger," the chief told me.

"That would be damn cool."

"It will happen someday, mark my words," he assured me.

I went over the boat and checked that everything was operational. I was just finishing checking things out when the crew showed up. I went over everything the chief had told me and had them get ready to get underway. We topped off the fuel tanks and fifteen minutes later we were heading back toward base at half speed. I decided to keep the RPM's down until we had a chance to do an oil change.

At this speed, it was going to be dark by the time we got back to the base. I called the LT and gave him our ETA. I just hoped we didn't run into any ambush sites. I really didn't want to put a strain on the engines with break-in oil in them.

We finally reached our BO at 0215. I let the LT know we were back and headed off to get some sleep. Of course, that wasn't quite as easy. The soft beds and lack of noise was suddenly gone. I could tell the fighting near our base had intensified. The outgoing arty sounded loud and the crackle of small arms fire was more noticeable. You could easily pick out the AK-47's from the M-16's. Every once in a while, a Claymore would go off, so you knew someone was in close contact with Charlie.

At 0800 the following morning I went to see the LT.

"Glad you are back. Business has really picked up this last few days. Something big is coming. You probably heard how close the contact is," LT Ellis said.

"Yeah, it's pretty apparent."

"Well Tet is in nine days and I'm guessing they are getting ready to push a big offensive. Our boats are a thorn in their rear and I think they want to do something about it," he replied.

"Do you think they will try to hit the base?"

"More than that. I think they will do everything in their power to take out the boats as well as the base."

I let this sink in a few minutes before speaking, "We need to send three or even four boats out at a time," I told him.

"I agree, but even that may not be enough. I am going to have the flyboys sitting in their choppers and ready to go at a moment's notice. They will piss and moan but I want them to be Johnny on the Spot if you get ambushed."

"I'll make up the assignments sheets. My guys are doing an oil change but once that is done we will be ready to go. I'll have Conway, Parker, and Willis as one patrol team. The new guy that replaced Keller is Morris. Him, Catcher, and I will make up the second team.

"Alright but that still leaves us pretty thin not to mention that it leaves hardly anyone to defend the base," the LT said.

"We need to get some help in here," I said, stating the obvious.

"I'm working on it."

There was nothing else to say so I headed back to the boat to have them get a move on. I went and told the three boat Captains; Conway, Parker, and Willis, about the patrol changes. When I finished with them I gathered up Morris and Catcher and went over how I wanted us to operate.

I wanted only one boat to do the stop and shop while one of the others covered the stern and port side and the other the bow and starboard side. I didn't want someone popping up with an RPG or AK and start blasting away. We would switch off from time to time to keep everyone sharp.

The first crew of Conway, Parker and Willis headed out and I stayed in constant contact with them. They ended up in a small tributary where two sampans were lurking.

"Don't screw around. Fire over them and if they don't submit to a search, take their ass out," I told them.

"Are you kidding me? They are trying to run," Conway informed me.

"Stop. Don't follow them. Just take them out from where you are. It has to be an ambush. They know they can't outrun you."

"Copy," he said and I could hear them unloading on the sampans.

"Ambush," Willis shouted over the microphone.

I just waited. The last thing they needed right now was for me to distract them from the chore at hand. Finally, Conway came back on the horn.

"Frickin' gooks. You were right. They had some heavy shit waiting for us along with RPG's. Good call Iceman," he said.

"Glad you guys are all right. Are you going to go ashore to investigate?"

"Yep. I'm covering Willis and Parker's crew. They are going to have a look see," he told me.

"Copy. Just be careful," I told them.

When he came back on the line he informed me that had found twenty RPG's, six hundred 7.62 x 39 rounds and twenty-one AK's. Not a large haul but anything that kept weapons out of the hands of the VC was a victory.

"You want us to bring the stuff back?"

"Can't see any reason to. Document it and toss the crap in the water," I replied.

"Roger. We will dump the stuff and continue our patrol."

"Copy that."

I didn't hear from them again until they called in a sit-rep reporting they were heading back to base. That was our clue to get ready to relieve them on our patrol.

CHAPTER FIFTEEN

We headed out shortly after the other boats got back. They told us that they heard lots of firefights going on, way more than usual. I took that to mean a major offensive was coming and Tet was less than a week away. I was already working on a plan for handling the gook's New Year's celebration.

The other patrol had been correct in their assessment. The intensity of firefights was increased. Our 155's howitzers were firing almost non-stop. Fast movers were dropping iron bombs and napalm at a furious pace. Black smoke rose in long rows as they released their deadly ordinance. A light fog of napalm smoke hung over the water and you could smell the liquefied petroleum it's made from.

We approached every boat with more caution than ever before. Each boat had the potential to be the last one we ever checked. Everyone was skittish.

Everything was going well until around noon. We had stopped two sampans close to the shore. Dog was going to go aboard and check the cargo of the first boat when the shore erupted with AK and the VC version of our light machine gun (M-60) the DP 7.62. Tex, Dog and Quacker immediately started retuning fire along the shoreline. Morris had his men blow the hell out of the two sampans.

The three of us immediately started circling the area the concentrated gunfire was coming from and let loose with everything we had. We were in a real dogfight, and more and more VC seemed to be cropping up with each pass.

"We need the choppers," I yelled over the microphone.

"Rodger that. Location?"

I gave him the coordinates and told them that we were up against a serious force.

"Any estimate as to how many?"

What? Did he think I was going to count the muzzle flashes coming from the shore? Geez, what a dumb question.

"A billion or so," I said sarcastically.

"A billion?"

"Just get the choppers in the air," I replied and went back to the business at hand.

All three of us were concentrating on where the DP 7.62 were firing from.

I thought I saw four of them spewing out their deadly rounds. You could see the rounds as they hit the water, at times walking their way towards the boat. That's when the captain must know his stuff. You would need to adjust speed or make corrections to direction to avoid getting the ship raked.

I was just starting a turn when I saw Catcher's boat lift up in the front and then suddenly just stop. It seemed to be drifting and I headed toward his boat as fast as we could go. The back end had taken an RPG strike. Hell, I didn't even see anyone shooting the damn things.

I pulled alongside and Dog and Skeeter jumped in the stricken boat. Tex threw a line over and made it fast. As soon as that was done I started pulling them away from the shore. I heard the Woosh of an RPG but I didn't even bother to look. There was nothing I could do about it at this point.

A huge geyser leaped up in the air just in front of Catcher's boat. Dog had grabbed hold of the M-60 on the boat and was blasting away. It was a pretty gutsy move considering how slow we were moving and our boat was relatively safe because we were shielded by the other PBR.

A second and third RPG landed near us and just as I was thinking they would zero in on us two big beautiful Hueys came in riddling the shoreline with machinegun fire and rockets. They poured it on until the shoreline fire subsided. I saw the door gunner give us a little wave as they peeled off back to base. I hate to admit it but they saved our ass.

Dog jumped back in our boat when we stopped.

"Bad?"

"Bailor, Parson, and Kingston are dead. Catcher is in bad shape. Took a round to the gut. We need a dust off immediately or he won't make it."

I got on the horn and relayed the information. The closest choppers were the two that helped us so they were dispatched back to get Catcher. I Jumped over in the other PRB and helped get Catcher in the basket so he could be airlifted. There was no need to hurry with the other three. We stacked their bodies in the cabin and re-positioned the bow of Catcher's boat so we could tow it back to base.

I gave the LT a quick rundown and we headed back. No one said much as we made the journey back to our home base. Three KIA, one WIA and just barely hanging on. Not one of our better patrols. One thing for sure, the aggression had taken a huge leap forward.

When we docked, I went to see the LT and gave him a verbal report.

"It's been like that all night and day. I have been getting non-stop reports of contact in almost every area. The VC are obviously planning something really big for Tet."

Just then two Phantom F4B's roared overhead on their way to a strike. Damn, nothing will inspire confidence like seeing those birds arrive and hit their target.

"Sir, I been thinking about our defense of the base. Obviously, they know we are here and I doubt they are going to just pass us by. I...

"Hold it son. I know you are just trying to help but give me a little credit. I've been working on this for a long time," the LT replied.

"Yes sir. Sorry sir. I just looked around and realized how vulnerable we are at the moment."

"Let me show you what I have planned and you can chime in as necessary," he said laying out an oversized map of the complex.

"Three rows of barbwire will be set up all around the complex. Inside the second one we will place Claymores. A trench will be behind the last row and all the support people will man those stations. Four of the boats will back up to the shore so they will have a good sweeping angle and can overlap coverage. The other three will nose into the shore to cover any attack from the far shore or any sampans that try to infiltrate the base. The two choppers are armed and ready at a moment's notice. They will move around each night so Charlie can't zero in on them. I just received two StarLite night vision scopes for Carson and Little. Carson has a Remington M 40 and Little is using a M21. They will be on top of the CP rotating at night to make sure no enemy try to get through the wire and remove or turn the Claymore mines back towards us."

I studied the map for several moments before replying.

"What about the front gate. That looks the most vulnerable area to penetrate."

"I agree. I haven't worked out that part yet, but I am looking at options," the LT admitted.

I finally said, "We could triple row the area with Toe Poppers. Really saturate the area. Of course, we would have to mark where everyone is located, but it would sure stop a bunch of VC."

"We captured a lot of RPG's as well, I guess we could give them a taste of their own medicine," the LT added.

"We could also take a couple of the M40 machine guns from the PBR's and set up a fallback parameter. We would need to space them far enough apart that they have overlapping kill zones and one hit wouldn't take them both out."

"Good. Good. Okay, let's get this done," he said and slapped me on the shoulder.

***

For the next two days, all patrols were suspended and we spent our time digging a trench, removing the machine guns, and relocating them, burying 300 toe poppers, and stringing barbed wire. I swear we had more injuries from working to fortify the base than we did while on patrol.

Each night the LT and I would go and inspect the work that had been done during the day. We were brutally critical of everything we came across. We were talking about life and death and the last thing we could afford was to do something half-assed.

After the third day, we sat down on top of the CP and just looked around. Occasionally, the whiff of marijuana would come our way but the LT was cool. He never said a word about it. There were more important things to worry about.

"One thing about it, you can sure see the stars at night in this God forsaken place," he said quietly.

"It would be really peaceful if it wasn't for the damn mosquitos and firefights," I said laying back, "I honestly can't understand what we are doing here. I mean, I know all about the communist and the domino effect, but we aren't doing anything but killing each other. We never gain any foothold. We have a fire fight, go away and a few days do it all over again. So, what's the real goal? I have to tell you, the Vietnamese people we stop on the river have no love for us. We are just something else to make their life harder," I said.

We just lay there looking up at the stars for several minutes not saying a word. Each lost in his own thoughts.

"You know, sometimes you just have to believe that the people above you know what they are doing. They see a much bigger picture than we do here in our little corner of the war," the LT finally said.

"I understand all of that, but they are not here with us. They have no idea what it's like. They don't see the resentment in the eyes of the people we stop. They are back in their air-conditioned trailers, eating hot meals every night and handing out medals to themselves."

"That's an oversimplification, but I understand where you are coming from. Still, someone knows why we are fighting the war this way," he insisted.

All I said was, "Right."

I headed to my hooch and the LT went back to the CP. In some ways, I wish I had never begun to question why we were there involved in a civil war between the two factions. I mean, it was just a war between the North and the South. I know we would have been resentful if some other nation had intervened in our civil war.

CHAPTER SIXTEEN

Something woke me out of a sound sleep. I lay on my cot listening, trying to figure out what was different. I got up, put on my boots, and walked out of the hooch in my skivvies. The LT and a half-dozen others were all standing there looking around.

"LT?"

"Weird huh?"

"No guns. None at all. What does that mean?" I asked.

"Not sure. Maybe they have withdrawn back into Cambodia," someone offered.

"Not likely," the LT said, and headed to the CP.

The LT had a company personnel man we called Mike the Monkey Man. He had been a Ham operator for several years before being drafted. He had erected an elaborate tower that he could turn by hand to pick up other stations. He had used the components of a Prc-25 radio and who knows what else to listen in to other outpost conversations. I had no clue as to how he had accomplished that feat, but it worked and allowed the LT to get additional information.

After a few minutes, LT Ellis came back to tell us that almost all contact with the enemy had ceased. IV Corps wanted everyone on high alert and all outpost to be fully maned in case a full-blown attack was coming our way.

We immediately placed the PBR's in position and moved the machine guns into place. The slicks moved to a different location. At dusk, they would move again and we would re-locate the machine guns. Our only real defense was to keep moving our assets around so they could not pre-register our positions. We kept the men out of the trenches until after dark so they wouldn't know their location.

There was nothing else we could do at this point except to be ready at a moment's notice. The LT moved onto my PBR along with Mike. The CP would be one of the first targets they would try to hit.

The night wore on and absolutely nothing materialized. We had all been so keyed up that it felt like a huge let down when nothing happened. All the next day we grabbed as much sleep as possible knowing that a major offensive could well happen at any time.

Another night went by and it was the same thing. Nothing happened. The jungle was the quietest it had ever been since my arrival. During the day, even the river traffic had almost come to a halt. Sporadic sampan would go by and if we sent one of the boats out, it was always the same. They would be loaded down with their families. Their destination was always to visit other relatives.

The Delta is their lifeline. Moving food was a way of life for them and now suddenly no food except for small amounts and loaded to the gills with family. Some were so low in the water you wondered why they didn't swamp and just sink.

The following night we were really tense and keyed up. It was January 30, 1968, and we were all hunkered down wondering if all hell was going to break lose or this would just be another sleepless night.

I was walking with the LT to the boat after making rounds to ensure that everyone was awake and alert. Just as I was about to say, 'I think we are as ready as we will ever be', I heard an incoming mortar round. I grabbed the LT and pulled him to the ground. Everything seemed to happen at once. A mortar hit the CP and AK's opened up. I saw what looked to be a thousand gooks come charging out of the woods into the small clearing in front of the compound. Everyone started firing and red and green tracers crisscrossed as the two forces began trying to kill each other.

I ran to my PBR, half dragging the LT with me and jumped on board. My guys were already blasting away. I dropped to one knee and began firing my M-16. It was insane. We could see hundreds of the VC falling before they even reached the barbed wire barrier. Once they made it that far our guys were cutting them down and they hung grossly across the barrier.

A couple of sappers were able to blow holes in the wire and others didn't hesitate to rush through only to be killed instantly. In the back of my mine I registered our people screaming and some yelling for a corpsman. The choppers were already in the air and making passes at the VC in the open. I could see tracers raining down and rockets blowing bodies into the air.

Just as I had expected, the VC had placed soldiers on the other side of the river and they opened fire. I was glad we had arranged three of the boats to point in that direction. That gave us six .50cal. machine guns to deal with that diversion.

The VC had made it inside the second row of barbed wire when I heard the claymore's go off. It ripped through them leaving half bodies hanging on the wire. I have no idea how many we had killed or how many men we had lost but the fighting continued.

RPG's were being exchanged as well. I'm sure it confused them for some time. Americans weren't known for RPG attacks. While all of this was going on I realized one of our M40 machine guns was no longer firing. I jumped off the boat, sloshed ashore and ran across the compound with bullets zipping around me. I jumped in the trench and landed on two of our guys. Both were dead so I just shoved them out of the way and started firing the gun.

A mortar round exploded just a few yards from me and damn near busted my ear drum. Dirt rained down on me. Another one hit close enough to literally knock me over. I would have bolted back to the boat but I saw a line of gooks heading for the entrance to the compound. This was still the weakest area in my mind. I opened fire as they came racing forward. It was like rats in a New York sewer. You killed five and ten more followed. Just then the first of the toe poppers went off followed by five, ten, twenty more. Bodies were blown apart and flung into the air.

No matter how many we killed, they kept coming. The slicks were firing non-stop and I continued to fire until I ran out of ammo. Staying there wasn't really an option but running back across the compound didn't have all that much appeal either. They were still running across the landmines but it wouldn't be long before they had cleared a path. I had to go.

I grabbed my M-16, crawled out of the trench, and ran hunched over toward the boat. I saw dirt kick up around me and knew someone would either zero in on me or a lucky shot would hit me. I made it to what was left of the CP and hunkered down. It was still a good fifty yards to the boat.

It was obvious that the Hueys were out of rockets so they were making passes so the door gunners could at least keep as many at bay as possible.

I glanced at my watch, I'm not sure why, but was surprised the firefight had been raging for almost two hours. Most firefights were short lived. I decided to make a mad dash for the boat and took off running as fast as my legs would carry me. I slipped on the bank and fell face first into the water but hopped back up and scampered aboard.

"Thought you had bought it when you went down like that," the LT said as he continued to fire his weapon.

"I just wanted to wash the sweat off me before coming aboard," I shot back.

Just then we heard a loud shrill of a whistle being blown over and over. The VC continued firing but began to fall back.

"What the hell? We couldn't have held them much longer," Ellis said.

"I guess they are going to regroup and try again," I answered.

Ellis said, "The sun will be up soon. You really think they will try it again during the daylight hours?"

"Hell if I know. All I do know is that we need to make repairs to the fence and mine field, get our remaining ammo handed out, find out who is KIA and WIA."

"You start taking care of that. I'll see if Mike can contact IV Corps."

"Aye, Aye Lieutenant," I replied and headed out to make the rounds.

***

The sun was up by the time I reported back to the LT. I gave him a full report of everything I found. We had three KIA's and five WIA's, that needed a dust off asap. The slicks were loading the remainder of the rockets, re-fueling, and re-supplying. I had everyone else making repairs and putting in the rest of the toe poppers. We only had a few more Claymores so we faced them where the main force had attacked.

"Who are the KIA's?"

"James Crumb: PO 3, Signal-man, Andrew Wilson: Seaman and Eddy Goleman: PO 3, Gunners Mate."

"I had just put Wilson in for a rate bump to 3rd Class PO."

"What about a dust off?"

"Mike is already working on it. Seems that almost every place was hit last night including Saigon. IV Corps is under attack," he said.

"No way."

"From what Mike pieced together they hit everything from all the way North to Quang Tri, all along the coast, and every major base and city in the south. Saigon is in real trouble from what he was able to pluck out of the radio chatter."

"Saigon? Man, what the hell is going on? I thought we had them on the run? The President said there was light at the end of the tunnel. For who? Them or us?" I said.

"We need to be ready. They aren't about to let us just stay here. They lost too many to just give up now. They don't seem to mind playing the attrition game," Ellis replied.

"We need a fallback signal to have people gather at the river's edge. We can attach some rafts to the boats to have people load in them if we start to get overrun. We'll pile as many into the boats as possible, load the rest in the rafts and head down river," I told him.

"Okay, do it," the LT said.

It wasn't the best solution but it was the only one I could come up with. I sure the hell didn't want to be taken prisoner and I doubt any of the others did.

I spent the next two hours going around, shoring up weak areas and explaining the fallback plan. The signal would be a flair from my PBR.

That meant to fall back to the shore. If we couldn't hold them off from there I would shoot a second flair and everyone would scramble on board or in a raft and we would bug out. The choppers were to take off as soon as the second flair went up as well.

I felt sorrier for them than I did for us. I honestly didn't know where they would go if all the bases were being hit. They would already have limited fuel and trying to find a place to land would be a major problem.

No dust-off's could be arranged due to all the causalities from the DMZ down to our area. Thirty-six major capitals had been hit and Khe Sanh was under siege.

"What about using one of our choppers?" Mike asked.

"That would leave us with only one to help defend. On top of that, just where would he go? For now, we just have to do the best we can with what we have," Ellis replied.

It sounded heartless, but he was definitely right. If one of the choppers left it would undoubtedly result in more KIA and WIA. We need them to help hold back the tide of VC that would be thrown at us.

Mike took off his earphones and said, "It sounds bad everyplace. There are NVA in the streets of Saigon and they are fighting from house to house. There is an attack underway on the US Embassy. They are blowing holes in the complex walls."

"Holy crap. Guys, I think we are in for the fight of our lives when they attack again," Ellis said.

No one disagreed.

CHAPTER SEVENTEEN

By 0200 everyone was so tense you could almost taste it. Even the mosquitoes seemed to realize something was up and stayed away for the most part. No pot smoking tonight, everyone was just hunkered down. They were all reminded not to smoke because the gooks could smell American tobacco a mile away.

I was back on the machine gun facing the front entrance. A guy named Larry Beal was with me to help load the gun. Earlier we had changed some of the toe poppers to concentrate more of them during the first fifty feet of the entrance. We also added two more rows of barbed wire that they would have to go through.

I was sitting on my helmet eating a C-rat when the whistle sounded. Damn, I was just getting ready to eat my pound cake, the best part of the meal. I put my helmet on, racked the machine gun, and got ready.

"Ready?" I asked.

"And if I'm not?"

"Good point," I said, thinking I was a dumb ass for even saying that.

Just like the night before, they came in a wave, hundreds of them all racing toward the barbed wire fence. I waited until the first one was about ten yards from the outer fence and opened fire. I traversed steadily from right to left then from left to right. Beal was good at his job and kept feeding the machine gun as well as anyone I had ever worked with.

Just like the night before, they didn't seem to mind how many we killed, they just kept coming. Once again, the slicks were raining down death from above with guns and rockets. We held them up at the outer fence until they finally managed to get the sappers close enough to blow holes in it.

The Claymores took out a large swath of them and set them back for only a minute or so before they resumed their push forward.

"Time to go," I told Beal and we sprinted for the boat.

When I got aboard I grabbed the flair gun and shot it into the air. Most of the men started immediately back to the shoreline. A few were so engrossed in the battle they didn't even pay attention. Trying to yell over the noise was impossible.

I jumped into the water and started to rush forward but Ellis caught me by the back of my jacket and yanked me off my feet.

"What in the hell do you think you are doing?" he screamed.

"I need to tell the others to fall back," I said trying to free myself from his grip.

"Get the hell back on the boat," he said.

"I can't, I have to tell them," I said, and pulled myself free.

I could hear him yelling at me as I took off running toward the trench where men were hunkered down firing at the onslaught of VC starting to breach the last fence.

I jumped in beside them and started pulling them and yanking on them.

"Back to the beach. Go. We are pulling out," I screamed at them.

The look in their eyes was unhuman. Wild and darting, like they didn't understand a word I was saying.

"If you stay here you will be killed or captured. Let's go. When I leave, you had better be right behind me," I shouted at them then turned and rushed down the trench.

I didn't even look back to see if they were following me. I had passed along the message and now it was their choice. At the end of the trench I jumped up and sprinted to the shore. A wounded sailor was lying face down with part of his right arm missing. I picked him up without hardly slowing down and kept on running as fast as I could. I hadn't even thought about how inviting a target I made to my own men, but fortunately, the LT had already told them to hold their fire.

Two of the men from the forward trench were running with me but two others had stayed. I could hear them firing and a few seconds later there was only the chatter of the Ak's. We watched from the shoreline as the VC rushed into the compound, firing into hooch's and any hiding place they could find. The slicks were still firing and were now hitting the compound itself. There was no way we could hold them off.

"As many of you as possible get on board the boats. The rest of you get in one of the rafts. We will tow you behind us," I screamed so everyone could hear me.

They began to get aboard but it was mass confusion. The boat captains were trying to get everyone situated, but a panic was starting, and everyone was shoving and pushing. These are the same guys that had been sitting in trenches while bullets and mortar shells landed all around them. I shot the second flair to let the choppers know it was time for them to leave.

The VC realized what was going on and began firing at our boats. We started the engines and some of the guys became frantic and started trying to swim out into the river. We pulled off the shore so only the life rafts were left. They had no choice but to settle down and get on board.

All the while the .50's were holding the VC back and finally we were able to slowly pull out from the shore and head down river. There was no way for them to follow us once we got around the bend in the river. Just as fast as the panic had started everyone relaxed and got their heads back on straight.

"Should I head for the Whitfield?" I asked the LT.

"Head that way. I think the Whitfield left, but some other ship will be there."

As we cruised along at a slow speed we could hear the roar of American artillery, see Phantoms dropping ordinance, and hear non-stop fire fights. I had never heard anything like it before. When we got to the basin outlet we headed toward the Whitfield.

It was totally dark and the ship had no lights on. We could just make out the silhouette as we were approaching. Suddenly, the water erupted as a mortar landed just a few feet from the ship. That was followed by two others both off their mark, but not by much. They would zero in within a few more shots. I could see that the ship was starting to reverse and was probably headed for deeper water out of mortar range. The smaller boats, PBR's, Swifts and others had been cut lose as the ship picked up speed.

Two more mortars landed right where the ship would have been just a few seconds ago. A third hit one hit one of the swift boats and within seconds it was sunk. Wisely, Lieutenant Ellis decided we should follow the ship and dock when it stopped. We didn't have to wait too long. They anchored a thousand yards or so further out.

We came along side and they lowered the ladder. The Lieutenant went aboard and a few minutes later returned and told me where to tie up the boat. Once that was done and the guys in the rafts were on board we were taken back to the crews bunk room. I took the same bed the last time I had been here.

I led everyone to the galley and was surprised at how full the of the crews were all setting around listening to the overhead speakers. Hanoi Hannah was giving a report on how the glorious North Vietnam soldiers were eliminating the imperial dogs. According to her, the Americans would soon be pushed into the sea and Vietnam would be reunited as Ho-Chi-Mien had envisioned it with his divine leadership.

We were all keyed up but eventually my adrenalin wore off just like what was happening to everyone else. We all drifted back to the bunk room and hit the rack just as the sun was rising.

***

I rolled out of bed at 1030 hours and sat on the edge reliving some of the events from last night. What the heck happened and why hadn't intelligence reports picked up about these attacks? When I got to the galley I learned that fighting was still going on all over South Vietnam. Saigon was under siege and the US Embassy's wall had indeed been breached. The radio station was now in the hands of the NVA and fighting was going on all over the city.

The same scenario was being played out from the DMZ to the Delta. Some outposts had been overrun and even some cities. It was hard to believe because we had all been told that North Vietnam had agreed to a seven-day cease fire to celebrate the Vietnamese New Year.

Ellis walked into the galley and motioned for me to follow him. We made our way to the fantail of the ship and leaned against the railing.

"We have a special mission. The other boats of all kinds are going to be taking part in an exercise to stop the flow of men and materials down the Ho-Chi-Mein trail."

"We won't be taking part?"

"No. We are going to take a special forces team to Prek Dambang."

"Never heard of it."

"No reason you should have. It's deep into Cambodia."

"Awe, you're kidding, right?"

"Do I look like I'm kidding? No this is a bonified mission. This came from the very top. I will be going with you, but you are the boat captain. I just wouldn't ask a crew to do this if I wasn't willing to do it right alongside of them."

"I appreciate that and I'm sure the men do as well, but LT, you have a different role to play. There is really no use for you to go along," I replied.

"No. I want to do this. I need to do this," he insisted.

Why? I mean, we are enlisted. We could be disavowed, but an officer is a slightly harder to dismiss. Still, he was the boss and if he said he was going I could do little about it.

"I need you to get your crew together and we are going to meet in the officer's mess at 1400 hours. No one will be there except for you, the crew and me. Time is short so we need to be ready to go by 2300 hours. Have the men get extra everything and we will be taking additional 55-gallon drums of fuel. I'll explain it all at the briefing," he said.

Crap. Crap. Crap. And that was all I had to say about that bit of news.

CHAPTER EIGHTEEN

I rousted everyone out at 1300 hours and had them put on clean uniforms since we were going to be in Officers' Country. We found the mess and I knocked on the door. The Lieutenant opened the door and we filed in.

"Take a seat, it would be better if you all sit on one side so you could review the map better," he said as he rolled out a familiar map of the IV Corps region.

"Is the boat ready to go?"

"Yes sir," I answered.

"Good. Now this is our destination," he said pointing to Prek Dambang.

Stunned silence, finally Dog cleared his throat and said, "Sir, that is pretty deep into Cambodia, right?"

"That it is. Our mission is to deliver a special forces team to that spot. Their mission is none of our business and neither are their names. Our job is to deliver them and bring them back. French and I are the only ones authorized to even speak to them. By the way, I will be going on this mission with you. Now here is the plan," he said hunkering down over the map.

We spent the next two hours going over every detail. Our major concern was obviously getting caught in Cambodian waters just like our earlier mission. Of course, the nagging small detail that we had to overcome was getting past Phnom Penn, the capital of Cambodia. Sure, no big deal. In reality, it was the most likely place for us to be spotted. I did not relish having to fight our way out of that area and back to Vietnam waters.

"Any more questions?" the LT asked as he was rolling up the map.

I was glad to see no one raise their hands. I know they had questions but now it was time to get the mission underway. There was a flurry of activity as my crew headed to the boat to go over every detail one more time. I'm pretty sure extra ammo was going to be loaded.

"What the hell?" I heard Quacker say to Tex.

I couldn't hear Tex's reply but there were a lot of cuss words.

Shortly before 2300 we all mustered at the boat and the Lieutenant went over last-minute instructions. Up until now he hadn't told us where we were picking up the special forces team.

"We will head upriver to Long Xuyen. They will be hiding along this area," he said pointing to the map, "They will signal with a flashlight. Three long, one short, two long. If it is a trap they will skip the one short," he told us.

"Okay," I said, looking at my watch, "I guess it's time to shove off."

"With the extra fuel, the LT, and the special forces team it was going to get crowded. I doubt we would be able to outrun any Cambodian patrol boats if we happened across them. At 2315 we shoved off and headed upriver. I was using half throttle once we planed out. The LT sat down on the deck and had his back against one of the 55-gallon drums.

Dog slid over to me and said, "Why is he coming along?"

"For a couple reasons. I think he wants to see what we actually go through. What it's really like out here on the river. The other reason is he feels he needs to get his hands dirty. He said he need to do it."

"You don't find that kind of weird?"

"Not really. To be an effective leader you can't just sit on your ass giving orders. You need to understand what the people under you are going through," I told him.

"They don't mind doing that in Washington," Dog replied.

"And that is why they don't have a clue as to how to really fight this war. They listen to Admirals sitting safety on ships or holed up in some fancy hotel in Saigon. Those guys aren't about to go out into the field and see what it is really like. Oh sure, they will get all kinds of medals for sitting on their fat asses but they sure don't deserve them. We are fortunate that our LT isn't like that," I told Dog.

We settled into our normal routine, all eyes watching the shoreline. We could still hear artillery fire and gun battles taking place all around us. Obviously, the VC offensive wasn't just a hit and run tactic like usual.

Two F-4 Phantom II streaked overhead, afterburners glowing blue as they raced toward their targets. Slicks were constantly making runs, tracers streaking down towards the ground.

"All hell is still breaking lose," Skeeter observed.

"This is the biggest sustained attack I have seen," Tex added.

"Look," Dog said, pointing to the sky.

"That's 'Puff'," the LT said.

"Puff? What is that?" Dog asked.

"A gunship with Gatling guns. It has three that can spit out 100 rounds a second. Think about that. Almost as fast as you can snap your fingers, one hundred rounds have been fired," he said.

"So, that red string coming down is what? Tracers?"

"Exactly."

"Damn. I sure wouldn't want to be on the receiving end of that thing," Dog replied.

"Its real designation is Spooky but most guys call it Puff the Magic Dragon because of the fire it spits out," the LT told him.

We all watched in fascination as the plane continued to send a lethal stream of bullets down. I realized we had all been watching Puff instead of the shore so I had everyone get back to watching the shore.

***

Two hours later Lieutenant Ellis came into the cabin and said according to his calculations we were getting close. I agreed, I had been thinking the same thing. We compared maps and decided we were just where we should be to start seeing the island, just off Long Xuyen.

"There," I said pointing to a clearing on the island.

Three long, one short, two long flashes. They were there and under no duress. I headed the boat into the area and within seconds they are on board. Our instructions were to not even speak to them, so I just backed the boat up and resumed our heading upriver and into Cambodia.

We were on the on the back side of the island the furthest away from Long Xuyen. Just as we were around the end of the narrow passage a shot rang out. Skeeter was standing on the stern just getting ready to pee, he suddenly toppled into the water.

Crap. A sniper must have been working the area. I wheeled the boat around so we could grab Skeeter. One of the Special Forces guys jumped up.

"Leave him. We need to get upriver," he ordered.

I ignored him and we headed for where Skeeter was bobbing in the water. He grabbed my shoulder and spun me around.

"I am ordering you to get going back upriver," he said, getting inches from my face.

"We are getting my crewman first. I don't know about you guys, but I don't leave my men behind," I said.

"Maybe you didn't hear me. That is a direct order."

"I don't give a rat's ass who you are. On this boat, I'm the Captain. Neither you nor any of your buddies have any authority over me. I out rank all of you and what I say goes. You don't like it, get out and walk," I said, and maneuvered the boat so Tex and Dog could get Skeeter out of the water.

"He is alive. The bullets a through and through on his shoulder. Probably has a broken shoulder blade but it could have been a lot worse.

With him on board and Dog tending to him, I turned and floored the boat clearing the area before the sniper could line up another shot. I could see the Special Ops guy talking to his men, but I just let it go over my head. Once were upriver some ways I throttled back and resumed our normal speed.

While we were cruising along the same guy came up and said in a low voice, "This isn't over yet. I'm a Major and I will have your ass."

"Let's see. I'm in Vietnam, all hell is breaking lose, I could die tomorrow, and you want my ass? Oh, and you want to be picked up when your mission is over? Does that about sum it up? I mean, boats do break down, shit happens."

"Are you threatening me and my men?" he snarled.

"Heavens no, just like you didn't threaten me."

"Hey," the LT said, "He is the Captain, just like he said. He outranks you when you are aboard. How about you cut the crap and just shut up, take a seat, and let us do our job."

He glared at both of us but finally went over and sat down.

"Gee, I hope we can find the spot where we dropped them off again," the LT said, just loud enough for them to hear.

***

Once we entered Cambodian waters you could feel the tension level take a leap. I think we were all surprised that we had heard fire fights still going on all the way up to the boarder. The VC must have launched a massive attack. The last time we were up here it was quiet. The sun was starting to come up and I began looking for a spot to hole up until dark.

I finally found a small inlet that we could nose into with the 50's out. Once we tied off to the trees on either side, we started the time-consuming task of camouflaging the boat. I had already decided that the 50's would be manned as long as we were tied up. I set up a two-on-two off watch. The last thing I wanted was for someone to fall asleep or start daydreaming. I took a watch as did the LT

The Special Ops guys just stayed huddled together playing cards and mumbling. I, for one, would be happy to see them go. They were nothing like the LRRPs we had brought up to Cambodia. They weren't so frickin' full of themselves like these jerks.

I figured if all went well we would be dropping them off at Long Xuyen around 0200 hours. We would have to find a place nearby to wait.

The plan was for them to take a day to get to the operation zone, a day to do the job, whatever it was, and a day to get back. We would observe radio silence until they were ready to be picked up. If all went well, we would be headed back down river long before the sun came up. The key being if all went well.

CHAPTER NINETEEN

We left just as soon as I felt it was safe. We headed upriver once again, hopefully on the final leg to letting our guests go about their job. There was a lot of cloud cover so I felt a little less exposed. In fact, I thought it might just rain and that would be unusual for this time of year.

We traveled along at half throttle and saw nothing suspicious. Most of the noise from fighting was behind us now. Skeeter was doing alright for a guy with a broken collar bone and a hole through his shoulder from back to front.

Dog had been taking care of him most of the time and doing all he could for him. If we were in Vietnam waters I would have had him sent to Saigon for medical treatment. Where we were now, it wasn't an option.

At 0235 by my watch we were approaching Phnom Penn, the capitol of Cambodia. We stayed on the far bank, but you could see the city lit up from a mile away. I slowed the boat so that we were barely making ten knots. I figured the less noise and wake the better. I was thankful for the dark skies.

Just as we approached the outer limits of the city it started to rain. Softly at first but it continued to intensify. Someone must have been looking out for us. Not only would it obscure vision but it would drive most of the Cambodians inside. I dropped the speed a little further as the rain intensified to the point that vision was even more obscured on the dark and moonless night.

I was more than relieved when we finally made our way around the bend and behind the lee side of the Koh Dach Island that divides two sides of the Mekong River. Once clear of the island I increased our speed and we headed deeper into Cambodia.

I shut the engines down while everyone helped with the refueling. The sun was only an hour from coming up and we needed to finish and find a safe place to layover until nightfall before finishing the trip and dropping off the Special Operations guys.

The refueling took longer than I had hoped for and we only had a few minutes before sunup. I had hoped we would have made it further and would be dropping off our cargo tonight, but that wasn't going to happen. I found a smaller place than I thought we really needed, but time was up. I nosed the boat in and everyone hustled to get the stern covered as fast as possible. Once that was accomplished we started working on the rest of the boat. We were making more noise than I would have liked, but time was of the essence.

We had no more finished when the first boats started to appear. Unlike Vietnam, there were usually just fishermen or people taking crops to market. At least that is what it appeared to be. I saw no one in traditional VC or NVA uniform.

We all hunkered down to do little more than wait out the day. The rain had stopped and now the sun was starting to bare down on us. With the 55-gallon barrels of fuel, extra personnel, and larger than usual supply of ammunition, there was not much room to spread out and very little shade other than what we had managed to put over the boat.

Anytime you are miserable and waiting, time seems to stand still. I must have looked at my watch a hundred times and I swear the seconds took an hour to move. We could do nothing more than clean weapons, eat and, sleep. Finally, the sun started to settle and we all began to come to life again. I had been studying the charts with the Lieutenant and estimated we would arrive at Prek Dambang around 0200 hours. The Special Ops leader came over and I explained how it was going to work. He just nodded his head.

"As I understand it, you estimate your mission will take three days, is that accurate?" I asked him.

"Affirmative."

"We will pick you up when you squawk at the same location unless you squawk twice for the 'B' site, which is the first fall back location. If you squawk three times we pick you up at the 'C' location which is the third fall back site."

"Affirmative," he replied.

"Alright, I will drift in, bow first, and your people can unload and we will head out to hide until we hear from you," I said.

He nodded again and went back to his men.

"Nice talking to you," I mumbled.

***

We uncovered the boat at 2300 hours, and I started out. It was another moonless night but so far it wasn't raining. I pulled out into the river and we headed up country, deeper and deeper into Cambodia. I looked at my watch and saw the Special Ops guys gathering on the bow.

"Over there," the Lieutenant said, pointing.

I headed to the landing point and idled the engines when we got close to the shore. When the boat hit land, the Special Ops guys hustled over the side and made their way ashore. Within seconds, they were gone from sight and I was backing the boat off the landing site.

I was in less of a hurry this time so I made sure I could locate a spot that offered us good coverage and the ability to break out in a hurry if necessary. There was an island opposite Prek Dambang that I explored before finding a small cove that we could get into and cover the boat extremely well. I backed in this time for a quick getaway if necessary. We had time to use some of the tree branches to build a cover over the bow to get out of the sun.

The Lieutenant sat down beside me in the wheelhouse and broke out a C-rat. It was as good a time to eat as any. I got beanie-weenies and went back to sit it on the manifold to heat it up. Most of the others had done the same thing. The LT was just eating the fruit cocktail and not bothering with the rest. When I looked to see what he had opened it was the dreaded ham and lima beans. No wonder he had just settled for the fruit cocktail.

My D-1 C-rat had peaches so I offered them to the LT. He gratefully accepted them. I always thought we should force the VC to eat the ham and lima beans to get them to talk, but I think that is against the Geneva Convention and considered cruel and unusual punishment.

I sat and talked to the Lieutenant and found that he was originally from a little town called Glendive, Montana. He had spent most of his life there until he went to Montana State University at the Flagship Campus. He had majored in Political Science and had given thought to becoming a teacher.

Ellis was easy to talk to and we got to know each other well on this trip. We even had a couple of debates about the war and why it was being fought. I was more cynical than he was. He believed if we didn't stop communism in Vietnam it would lead to the fall of Cambodia, Thailand, and Laos. He was sure, too, that the Chinese had designs on the entire region.

He could be right but where we really differed was the way we were fighting the war. I was totally opposed to fighting the VC for a piece of worthless land one day and then giving it back the next day.

"Look, we can't win the war this way. If we are going to win we need to have our hands untied and let us get the job done. Bomb Hanoi to rubble and any other city of size. Stop fighting for control of South Vietnam and pound North Vietnam until there isn't anything left," I argued.

"And kill innocent people?"

"Hell, they do it every day along with our guys. We can't win by attrition. They won't stop fighting. We are in their country, and they won't quit until the last one is standing. We have to cut them off at the knees if we want to win."

"And do you think China would just stand by and let that happen? What about Russia? They are getting rich supplying them with weapons. They want the war to go on. It's good for their economy," he argued.

"It is helping our economy as well. All the fat cats that make weapons are getting rich with our blood," I replied.

"You're missing the bigger picture. The Communists want to take over the world. America is the only nation that can stop that from happening."

"Then let us stop it. Do whatever is necessary to kick them out of Vietnam. Just totally unleash our military. No rules of engagement, no restrictions on where we can and can't drop bombs. Bring as many fighting men as necessary to get the job done. Right now, all we are doing is playing their game. We need to take the initiative and bring this war to an end. How many more soldiers have to die in this war of attrition before we decide to call it quits?" I said.

"We won't call it quits. We are in this for the long haul. It may take a longer time than expected but we will get it done," the LT replied.

"Sorry but I disagree. We won't get it done if we keep playing by rules. You can't win a war by fighting on their terms," I insisted.

"We are a civilized nation. We can't just start killing innocent people in North Vietnam."

"Civilized? Since when did war get civilized. Are the VC civilized when they kill an entire village because they think they are pro-American? When they slaughter women and children? I don't see that as civilized. We should do exactly what they are doing. If we did that in the north, this war would be over in a year," I insisted.

We talked about the war effort for the next two hours but in the end, nothing was resolved. Maybe I'm a defeatist or not patriotic enough but I just couldn't see what we were dying for like this. Just turn us loose and we will kick ass.

I was pretty sure every enlisted man felt pretty much the same way that I did. It was hard to understand what we were really accomplishing in Vietnam. We should be taking the war to them instead of doing the fighting in South Vietnam. As far as I was concerned, screw the DMZ. Head into North Vietnam and level it if necessary. All the fear of Russia or China using nuclear bombs was a joke. They weren't any more likely to use them than we were. Saber rattling has been going on since the first war. MAD (Mutually Assured Destruction) would keep all three nations from unleashing nuclear weapons.

CHAPTER TWENTY

After the Lieutenant went off to get some shuteye, Dog came over and sat down beside me.

"I overheard you talking to the LT. You are right. This hit and run crap ain't ever going to get it done. Why we don't just wipe the gooks off the face of the earth is beyond me. If I had my way, I would shoot every one of them. They are all gooks and hate us. Shit, we shouldn't even be here. This isn't our fight. I mean when I first got here I was all gung-ho, but with thirteen days and a wake up, I can't see a damn thing we have accomplished," he said, drinking the syrup from his canned peaches.

"I'm sure some of them are good people but you're right about them not caring for us. You can see it in their eyes every time we stop one of their sampans," I told him.

"The only good gook is a dead one. Then I don't have to worry about them trying to kill me," Dog replied.

"Anyway, you only have a few more days...."

"Thirteen and a wake up," he interrupted, like I had forgotten that important bit of information.

"And you can go back to the real world. The question is; what are you going to do when you get back?"

Lake replied "Get the biggest steak I can find and the coldest beer and stuff myself. Get a chick and get laid,"

"Yeah, yeah. We all say that. I mean what are you going to really do? What kind of job?"

"Hell, I don't know. I haven't thought about that much. I mean, I'll find something to do. I can tell you one thing. I sure won't go home. I tried that once and I just can't relate to them any longer. They have become so weird. I can only be around them for a couple of hours before I'm ready to blow my brains out. They don't understand anything about what we go through over here. All they know is what the news tells them."

"What did you do before you enlisted?" I asked.

"Bummed around mostly. I worked for a landscaper for a while but the guy was a wetback and couldn't speak English worth a crap."

"Just keep you head down and don't do anything stupid for the next few days."

"You can bank on that," he replied.

I saw Skeeter lift his head and I went over to talk to him. He looked like crap but I sure wasn't going to mention it.

"Hey bro, how you hanging?"

"Not bad for a guy with a broken collar bone and a hole punched clear through me. I gotta tell you, it hurts like hell," he replied.

"Look Shelton," I said using his first name instead of Skeeter, "I will run this thing at full speed once the op is over. I know you hurt, but a few inches more and it would have been your head exploding. I know that doesn't take the pain away but I would rather have you hurting than dead."

"I know, and Dog has done everything he can for me to help with the pain."

"I know. He asked about giving you Morphine, but I honestly don't think it's a good idea. I told him to stick with the Naproxen and Tylenol. I'm hoping we have enough of the saline to last us until we get back," I replied.

"He is doing his best. He has changed the bandages four times and the bleeding has almost stopped. Dog is good people," Skeeter said.

I nodded agreement. I knew he was really hurting, but at this point there was absolutely nothing we could do. Keep him as comfortable as possible, but other than that, our options were limited. This is where being able to call in a dust off would really come in handy but being in Cambodia eliminated that possibility.

I had just gone up to talk to Tex when there was a blast so loud I put my hands over my ears. A shock wave caused some of our camouflage to become dislodged. It was followed by a continuous non-stop barrage. You knew it had to be from the US B-52 dropping bombs on the Ho-Chi-Mien Trail. I had heard them before, but never this close. I looked at the map and realized the trail was less than two klicks from where we were hiding. They seemed to go on for an hour but it was probably less. I can't imagine what it would have been like if you were on the trail when all hell broke loose. I also wondered how effective they were. After all they were dropping the bombs from over 50,000 feet.

It finally stopped and we all went back to what we were doing which was mostly being bored. Tex and Cracker were playing cards. They were playing Head's Up where you place the card on your forehead and bet on the lowest card.

"So, who is winning?" I asked.

Tex replied, "I am."

"Yeah but I'll get it all back," Cracker assured me.

"How much are you down?" I asked.

"Fourteen billion dollars."

"I see. Well that may take a little time to pay off at your salary."

"Nah. Just a couple of good cards and I am right back in it," Cracker replied.

I decided there was nothing more I could say so I went over and racked out. We still had three more hours of sunlight. I had only been asleep a few minutes when the LT put his hand over my mouth and woke me.

He pointed to an opening in our camouflage. Three sampans were slowly going by, each loaded with VC. Most were holding AK-47 but two had RPG's strapped on their backs. They were towing a fourth boat that looked like it was loaded down with ammunition. It would be a heck of a haul but there was nothing we could do about it except watch them head on down the river towards Vietnam.

Thirty gooks and a lot of weapons and ammo was hard to let pass.

We were all pumped with adrenalin and ready for a fight if they had seen us. Now they were heading on down river and we could only go back to sitting on our butts. It may seem strange to non-military people but the whole time you are in the service it is kind of like that. Something comes up and you start your motor running a hundred miles an hour and then it's over and you go back to being bored. It always seems to be one extreme or the other.

"That was painful to watch and do nothing about it," I said to the LT.

"Tell me about it. We can't even break radio silence to let someone down-river know they are coming. One of our slicks could make mincemeat out of them."

"We probably could have gotten them all. Of course, it would put the mission in jeopardy, but other than that," I replied.

"Yeah, other than that small detail. Wishing isn't going to make it so. We might as well enjoy the lull while we can," the Lieutenant said.

I decided this was as good a time as any to eat so I grabbed a C-rat and took my trusty P-38 opener and opened the lid. I got the beef but found it hard to get down cold. I took a little ball of c-4 and placed on the engine cover and heated it up. At least like that you could get it down, especially if you doused it in Tabasco Sauce. I got lucky and got the pound cake. That was always a treat.

Since only one person smoked you couldn't use them much for trading. I usually just gave them away. Well, except for the Camels. You could hardly get anyone to even take them. When I was done, I cleaned my spoon by just licking it and put it back in my pocket. I put my P-38 back on my dog tag chain.

I went over to Skeeter and checked on him. He wasn't looking very good. I was starting to wonder if he was going to be able to hold on until we got back.

"Hey buddy, how about I make you something to eat?"

"Not hungry."

"Look man, you have to eat to keep your strength up. I snagged some beanies for you and a can of peaches. It doesn't get much better than that."

"Maybe I'll try the peaches."

I opened the can and carefully stabbed one of the slices and placed it in his mouth. He closed his eyes and slowly chewed.

"Damn, those are good," he whispered.

"Come on. Take another bite," I said placing another one in his mouth.

I was thinking how something as simple as a sliced peach can be so good when you are out in the boonies. Peaches, pears, fruit cocktail and pound cake were like gifts at Christmas time. You didn't get them at every meal but when you did you felt like you had hit the jackpot.

He got about halfway through the can before he said he was finished. I was really worried about his health but there was absolutely nothing that any of us could do at this point. Dog came over and checked on him and just shrugged at me. We were both thinking the same thing.

CHAPTER TWENTY-ONE

It was another long night with nothing to do except sleep, but even that gets boring after a while. The one thing we had to look forward to was getting the mission over with tonight. We should get the signal and then we could pick them up and get out of Dodge. As crazy as it sounds, I wanted to get back to Vietnamese waters.

Sometime around noon a strange thing occurred. Probably a hundred dead bodies came floating by, all tied together. Obviously, someone had carried out a mass execution. There were women, children and old men all attached by a rope around their ankle. This was something I had never seen before. We were all looking through the foliage, not saying a word. When the last of them went by we just looked at each other.

"What the heck was that?" I asked.

"Probably the Khmer Rouge. They do that quite often. If a village doesn't produce or isn't responding the way Pol Pot thinks they should, he sends in troops for mass executions."

"Now that's hard core. Hell, while we are at it, we should wipe his ass out as well."

28

"I've only seen it a couple of times but it's always the same. Men, women, and children all tied together and floating down the river," the LT. said.

It made me reflect on how someone could be that evil. What would possess a person to just have a whole village murdered because he was pissed at the inhabitants? Surely the old men and kids hadn't done anything to deserve this. As much as I hated the VC, at least they were fighting to reunite their country. The Cambodian warlord seemed to just be doing it because he could and no one could stop him.

Once the last of them floated by, we all started to settle down when suddenly the radio crackled.

"Tango One, Delta One. We are pinned down and taking heavy fire. We need immediate extraction. One WIA and we are hold up at extraction point C. We need immediate withdrawal."

"What the?" the LT said.

"They must be in a world of hurt to broadcast in the open and during daylight hours. What do you want me to do?" I asked the Lieutenant.

"It's your boat and your crew. You should be the one to make the call. There is no real right or wrong."

Without another word, I fired up the boat and my crew immediately went to their combat positions. I didn't bother to remover the camouflage; I just jammed the throttles full forward. As soon as we cleared the cove, I made a hard-starboard turn and we shot up the river. Five or six sampans were on the water and you could see the shock registered on their face when we went full bore past them. The wake sent two of the boats toppling over, dumping the food and people in the water. Ten minutes later we were approaching the extraction zone.

Just as the LT was pointing to the spot, we started taking fire. Bullets were slamming into the hull, 50's tub and just about every inch of the boat. We all began firing at the flashes coming from the shoreline. It must have been a big force because we were getting hit no matter how much I tried to zig and zag.

I rammed the boat ashore and two of the Ops guys ran out dragging the third guy. They hopped on the boat and pulled the other guy onboard. I reverse thrusted and swung the boat down river. I was going to make for the far shore to cut down on the accuracy of their fire but just as I turned the stern an RPG plowed into our side and exploded when it hit the starboard engine.

The boat made a hard-right hand turn and I shut the throttle off on the disabled motor, spun the wheel to the port and continued heading as fast as possible across the river. A second RPG fell just short of hitting the same spot.

Once I got to the far bank we headed down river as fast as we could. It was a struggle because the boat had sustained some serious damage and the steering was sluggish and we sort of weaved down the river. I wasn't too keen of doing this in broad daylight either. Once we were out of firing range I throttled back and did a quick look around. That's when I saw the LT sitting on the deck holding his leg. His uniform was covered in blood. Quacker had already started compression on the wound and was wrapping a bandage around it.

"Morphine?" Quacker asked.

"What do you think LT?" I asked Ellis.

"If it wouldn't be too much trouble."

He tried to laugh but it turned into a grimace just as quickly. Quacker stabbed the needle in his leg and put his jacket under the Lieutenant's head.

"Skeeter and Tex bought it as well," he said.

"The RPG?"

"Yep."

"I kind of figured that when the back .50 quit firing," I said.

"Picking these yahoo's up in broad day light is the reason we are all shot up," Quacker said, gripping his M16 tighter.

"You know they wouldn't have called unless it was critical. You saw what they were up against. They only had a small patch of shore to try to hold out on. If we hadn't gotten there when we did, they would have either been captured or killed," I told him.

"How nice. We saved their asses but got ours shot off. I doubt if Skeeter and Tex would have thought that was a good trade."

I decided there was nothing I could say that would make it better. Quacker had been through a lot more with them than I had.

"Dog came over and sat down on the floor of the wheelhouse.

"That sucked," he said.

"We took a pretty good ass whipping," I agreed.

"Twelve and a wake up," he said and stretched out and covered his eyes with his boonie hat.

Within seconds I could hear him softly snoring. Sleeping had never been a problem for Dog. The Special Ops leader came back to speak with me.

"Our guy is pretty shot up."

"Yeah, I got two dead and the LT isn't going to be dancing for a while either."

"I'm sorry about your men. This whole thing was FUBAR. When we got to the target location, he wasn't even there. We ran into more Gooks than you can count. We were going to just go to the first extraction location and call you at night but we were discovered and we spent the rest of the time trying to evade them. We finally decided to try to hold them off until dark, but more and more kept pouring into the area and we ran out of real estate."

"Cambodians?"

"NVA"

"NVA? What were they doing over in Cambodia?"

"That's part of the FUBAR. Our mission had nothing to do with the NVA. We didn't even know they were there. No one briefed us on that little piece of intel," he said.

"Well, so far it has cost two KIA and two WIA counting your man and we are still in Cambodian waters and have a long way to go. Pretty high price to pay for faulty intel."

"I'm hip to that," he said and walked away to check on his wounded guy.

I was as tense as a cat surround by German Shepherds. Here we were struggling to get back to Nam waters in broad day light with a shot up boat that had only one working engine. By my calculations, we still had ten more miles to go before we cleared the border.

Just when I thought it couldn't get much worse I found it could. Not just a little, but a whole lot. As we rounded a bend in the river I saw a line of boats clear across a narrow section of the Delta. They were all sizes and shapes. It was obvious that their intent was to stop us. I didn't have to tell anyone to get ready. Quacker, Dog and the Special Ops guys were all in place.

I had already decided on a course of action. I figured the strongest point of the line would be in the center. I continued to head for that area. About three hundred yards out, I could see the water kicking up from the bullets. No RPG's yet thankfully. I continued for another few seconds and then wheeled to boat hard to port and then straightened out again. It would cut down on their ability to fire at us if we sliced through weakest link in the chain. A hail of bullets was being exchanges and I felt a searing hot piece of metal across my temple and ear lobe. It almost drove me to my knees but I stayed up right and steered the boat directly between two of the sampans tied together. I could see the men diving overboard as we rammed the boats at full throttle.

We hardly shuddered as we sliced right through them. The biggest problem was that the .50 on the stern had been knocked out so all we had were the M-16's. I zig-zagged as much as possible. As I looked over my shoulder I saw one of the Special Ops guys, sort of lift off his feet and fall hard to the deck on his back. Bullets were still dancing all around us as I tried to coax more speed out of the boat.

Finally, we were far enough away that we were out of danger. My ear felt like it was on fire and I reached up to feel it. Blood was running down the side of my face and I couldn't find the top part of my ear. There was just a patch of gristle flesh. I wasn't too worried about the amount of blood. Head wounds always bleed a great deal. It did sting like blue blazes, but it was nothing like what the LT was going through.

All things considered, breaking through the barrier they had thrown up could have been worse. We now had three KIA's and two WIA's but that could change if we ran into another ambush. It was a huge relief when we finally reached the border and were back in Vietnam waters. I didn't want to stop, but we were running out of fuel and were going to have to resupply from the last of the 55-gallon drums.

With just Dog, Quacker, the one Special Ops Major and myself, it took much longer. We finally finished just as the sun was starting to set.

One of the first things I noticed was that the fighting was still raging all around us. Choppers, phantoms, and the 155's, were still going strong. We could hear firefights taking place on both sides, all up and down the Mekong Delta. Whatever was happening, it was not the typical Charlie attack.

CHAPTER TWENTY-TWO

It started raining around midnight. We pulled the LT and wounded Special Ops man into the wheelhouse. Quacker stayed in the tub with his poncho on. We didn't have any body bags so the KIA we left on the deck. For the next two hours, the downpour was so intense that it was impossible to see the bank on the other side of the river.

We passed by our old base of operation and could see no movement. Evidently, the VC weren't interested in holding it in the long run. The only thing left standing of the structures was part of the dock. The maintenance facility had been burned to the ground. I wondered if we would come back and re-build or pick another spot for our operations.

As we continued down the river you could hear what appeared to be a huge battle raging in or near Saigon. Another seemed to be taking place a little further north, probably Bien Hoa.

We finally ended up in the South China Sea and I headed our battered boat toward the repair ship. We found the LST Harriet County, and reported we needed body bags and that we had serious damage. We were cleared to tie up by the crane so our boat could be lifted out of the water.

Before lifting the boat, they lowered a net with the body bags. We put our three KIA's in them and I removed one of the dog tags from Skeeter and Tex. I handed them to the Lieutenant who was next to be lifted up.

I was the last one to leave the boat. It was in pretty bad shape but had managed to get us out of Cambodia and all the way to the South China Sea. When I was inspecting the damage, I realized if the RPG had hit just three inches lower we would have sunk. I said a prayer of thanks for divine intervention.

As I came onto the main deck an officer stopped me and looked me over.

"You need to have that wound attended to," he said, indicating my ear.

"It's not so bad. Obviously, it could have been worse."

"It's bad enough. You need to get to sick bay and have them look at it."

"Can you tell me how to get to sick bay?" I asked.

"I can do better than that. I'll take you there."

"Thank you, sir."

"You just came off the boat they pulled out of the water, didn't you?" he asked.

"Yes sir. I'm the boat captain."

"I don't know why that thing is still afloat. Three KIA, two WIA is the scuttlebutt."

"Yes Sir."

"You had Seals on board. I saw them come off the boat."

I didn't reply.

"I get it. Well, at least you made it back. Sick bay is at the end of this passageway," he said pointing.

"Thank you, sir. I appreciate it," I replied and walked down to sick bay.

When I got inside a nurse came over to me and had me sit down.

"Wow. You lost a lot of that ear. I'm more concerned with the wound on your temple," she said getting a cloth with something on it to wipe off the blood.

She fussed around for several moments, checking out my scalp. She dabbed something on it that stung, but there was no way I was going to show it hurt.

"Tough guy, huh?" she said smiling.

It was right about then that I realized she was the first girl I had seen up close since being in-country. She wasn't a staggering beauty but she was wholesome and nice looking. More importantly, she was caring. Once she had me cleaned up she went to get the doctor.

"I'm Doctor Pointer. I would say you are lucky young man. Another inch and we wouldn't be having this conversation. The gash on your temple is pretty big. I need to put some stitches in it and then we will see what we can do about that ear. Babs, Get me a 3-0 suture packet and lidocaine. I'll scrub up and be right back. The ear is going to need more than a few stitches I'm afraid," he said.

"I'm Martin French," I said.

"Ensign Barbra Peterson," she replied.

"So, what does my ear really look like?"

She handed me a mirror and I was a little taken aback. The whole top quarter was gone. Just ragged skin hanging in a few places.

"Nice," was all I said.

Ensign Peterson cleaned my ear which made it hurt more than before. Doctor Pointer used lidocaine to numb the area and then stitched up my scalp. I'm not sure how many he put in but it felt like nine or ten.

"Now we need to work on that ear of yours. Lay back on the table. I'll numb the area and see what I can do with it," he said.

He poked and prodded for a while then they put a mask over my nose and mouth and that was the last thing I remember until I woke up in recovery.

When I came to, the doctor said, "You are going to have a doozy of a headache for the next couple of days. Ensign Peterson will give you some pain pills. Don't be a hero, take as many as you need. If you run out, come back, and get some more. I want you back here the day after tomorrow regardless. I want to keep a close eye on your scalp and ear. I don't want any infection to get started."

"Aye, Aye Sir," I replied.

"Good, Ensign, I'll leave him in your hands. Bandage his ear and scalp wound."

"Yes Doctor," she said as he turned and walked off to see another patient.

"Kind of abrupt," I replied.

"His bedside manner may lack but he is one of the best surgeons on board. He could leave the Navy and go into private practice and make a killing, but he is more interested in patching up the troops. He really is a hell of a doctor," she said, starting to work on my scalp and ear.

She smelled fresh and clean and I suddenly realized I must smell like something the cat drug in. I was in blood-soaked clothes and hadn't had a bath in four days.

"Sorry," I said.

"About what?"

"I know I kind of smell bad. This last mission kept us out for a while and I really need a shower and shave."

"You're fine. We get everything you can imagine in here so just relax. Tell you what, after I get you all bandaged up, you go take a shower, change clothes, and I'll meet you in the galley and you can buy me a cup of coffee," she said.

Whoa...I wasn't expecting that. I mean, I'm not the most debonair guy in the world and certainly not the most handsome. I did manage to get out that it would be an honor. I was blushing and she thought it was cute that I was nervous.

She gave me a shower cap that I was supposed to wear to protect my ear and scalp but I knew darn well I was going to wash my hair one way or the other.

I went back to my quarters and took a shower. I carefully washed my hair the best I could. I kept most of the water off the bandages but I couldn't keep it totally dry. I shaved and took an inventory while looking in the mirror. I looked silly with the big bandage on my ear. I could see that my face had more lines around my eyes that I had just six months ago. This place was taking its toll both physically and mentally. I wondered what I would be like by the time my tour was over.

Once I was cleaned up, I slipped into a set of clean dungarees and headed for the galley. The place was busy and I managed to claim two chairs at a long table that wasn't totally full. She was going to meet me at 1630 hours. I checked my watch and I was five minutes early. That was okay with me, I would rather be early than late.

1635...1640...1650...1700 all came and went and still no Ensign Peterson. By 1700 I was starting to get dirty looks and people poured in and all the places were filled. I still held on to the second chair.

At 1800 I decided she wasn't going to show. Either she had forgotten or an emergency had cropped up. I sighed and headed back to my bunk. I had really been looking forward to talking to someone about something other than the war. Honestly, I felt a little stupid for acting like a schoolboy that had been turned down for the prom.

I decided to go check on Lieutenant Ellis and see how he was doing. Secretly, I was hoping to run into Ensign Peterson, but no such luck. I checked in with the nurse and was told that Lieutenant Ellis had come through surgery just fine and that he would be transferred to Okinawa for recovery. I asked about the wounded Navy Seal, but she said she wasn't at liberty to give out any information on his condition.

This left me in both a funk and a quandary. I had no idea what would happen next. My boat was shot to hell, the base had been overrun, and my CO was going to be transferred. Adding all that up came to a big fat *zero*.

Dog and Cracker came over when I got to my bunk.

"What's the skinny?" Dog asked.

"Damned if I know. The LT is headed to Okinawa to recover. I don't know squat about our boat."

"So, what do we do?"

"Wait. I guess. Someone will come along and tell us what we are to do next."

"Well they had better hurry because I have ten and a wake up," Dog reminded us for about the hundredth time.

"I'm getting pretty short myself," Cracker added.

"Hell, you ain't short. You still have forty-two more days to go. I can't be talking to no lifer."

"Is to laugh, yuck, yuck. At least I ain't like the Iceman. What do you have? Six more months? Man, you are in a world of shit if the VC keep this kind of pressure up. They are getting serious about this war," Cracker said.

"I'm doing just fine."

"Right on, you keep believing that crap," Cracker said and drifted off to his bunk.

I undressed and hit the sack. I was still bummed out about Ensign Peterson standing me up.

CHAPTER TWENTY-THREE

The next morning, I put on my work clothes and headed to the mess hall to grab some breakfast. In all honesty, I was still hoping I would bump into Ensign Peterson. Cracker and Dog drifted in and joined me.

"Nine and a wake-up," Dog said while shoving pancakes loaded with syrup in his mouth.

"Got it Dog," I replied.

"You got to talk faster. I don't have enough time for long conversations," he retorted.

Man, it was going to be a miserable week if we had to go through this every morning and night. After chow, we headed up to see what was happening to our boat. We found it suspended from a sling and a Chief was walking around looking at it.

"You guys took a pretty good lick," he said, pointing to the stern, "A few more inches and none of you would be here."

"We lost three as it was," Cracker said.

"I know. I'm just saying."

"So, what's the plan?"

"I looked up your boat's records. You guys just had a major overhaul less than a week ago. We are going to have to do a hell of a lot more work on this baby. With what's going on all over the South, they want me to get you guys back into action. You are going to be given a different boat for the time being. Once we get yours repaired you will be able to switch back," the Chief told us.

"I'm going to need a crew. Dog only has a few days left and will be rotating back to the world. Cracker doesn't have that much longer either."

"Nine and a wake up," Dog interrupted.

"That's not my area. You need to go see the XO and see what he says."

"Assuming he gets a crew together, when will we get the other boat?"

"I can have it prepped and checked out in a couple of days," he replied.

"Then I should go see the XO right away."

The Chief pointed me in the right direction and I went to see him alone. There was no use in having Dog and Cracker tag along, besides, I didn't want Dog to say, 'nine and a wake-up' to the XO.

"Come" a deep voice said when I knocked on the door.

I stepped inside and stood at attention. He looked up and sat back in his chair. He was bald with muscles that seemed to want to pop right out of his uniform.

"Well Petty Officer first class, what can I do for you? And for goodness sakes, relax.

"Aye, aye sir," I replied.

"Well?"

"I'm the captain of the 991 PBR that came in yesterday..."

"Ah. The one with the KIA's. Yes, I heard all about the situation from Lieutenant Ellis. He spoke very highly of you. He said you were the reason any of them survived."

I'm sure my jaw dropped open. All I had done was what any captain would have done. Do the best you can to get out of a difficult situation.

"Sir, I..."

"Yeah, he said you would try to brush it off. You might as well know he put you in for a Bronze Star. I have the recommendation right here," he said holding up a paper.

I let out a big breath of air.

"So now you want to know what happens next. I haven't quite got that figured out. We can get you another boat, but getting a crew is the real problem. You are undoubtedly aware of the VC attacks all over South Vietnam. Saigon is still under attack as are many other cities. They caught us with our pants down around our ankles. Someone actually believed the little bastards would keep their word about the New Year's nonaggression agreement. The good news is that your home base is back under our command and is being rebuilt as we speak. They have sent a battalion of engineers to rebuild the base."

"That is good news. Sir, it seems kind of strange that no one caught the build-up. I mean we knew something big was coming almost a week before Tet. All the signs were there. Larger units, more NVA, increase in contacts, and just the feeling you get when you know the SHTF is coming."

"You knew, and so did probably a few thousand other groups, but the big brass doesn't really listen. They are in Washington, 6000 miles away trying to tell us how to run the war."

"And getting us killed in the process," I muttered.

"Listen, French, give me a day or two to line up a crew and then we can work out the details of who will be assigned to you."

"Aye, aye sir."

"Anything else?"

"Actually, there is. Reggie Keller only has ten days left. Could he be sent back and not used on any further patrols?"

"Sent back where? The whole country is in a world of hurt. I can keep him here on the ship until we can find a way to get him out of country, but that's all I can do for now."

"Yes sir, I understand."

"Sorry. Until this skirmish is over, everything is on hold."

***

A day or two turned into three and then four before the XO sent for me.

"The Chief said that he has a boat ready to go. Your boat won't be repaired for at least ten days or longer. We can't get the necessary parts out of Saigon. The city is still under siege."

"I'll take whatever he can come up with," I replied.

"Good. GM2 Fowler will go with you. You will have two new men. Signalman third class Clark and Seaman Baker. Clark was on another boat that was sunk and knows the drill. Baker is about two weeks in-country so he doesn't know much. He never got assigned a boat due to Tet."

"Having Fowler and Clark will make it a little easier."

"Hopefully. Now for the rest of it. You will be attached to III CTZ at Ben Keo while they finish your base," he said, walking over to a large map pinned to the wall.

"Ben Keo is located on the Vam Co Dong River, right here," he tapped the map, "The PBR's primary job isn't all that much different than where you were. Stop the flow of men and materials out of Cambodia. As you can see, Cambodia is just a hop, skip, and a jump away from where you will be operating. Your commanding officer will be Captain Willard and that's all I am going to say about that."

Man, I didn't like the way he said the last part. Where I operated from didn't matter much, but if Captain Willard was a stickler that went by the book, I wouldn't fit in very well. It was damn sure Cracker wouldn't. I was glad that Dog was not going to be sent out with us. He was down to five and a wake up.

He continued, "Ben Keo is an ATSB and you will be taking part in an operation called Giant Slingshot. You and the other PBRs will be engaging the VC and trying to put a stop to the flow of them out of Cambodia and into Vietnam."

"Aye, aye sir. When do we take off?"

"0700 tomorrow. I have Clark and Baker waiting for you in the galley. I told them to stay there until you showed up."

"Then I should go meet them and get the show on the road," I replied.

"No time like the present," he replied.

When I left the XO's quarters I went to the bunk room and found Cracker racked out. I woke him up and gave him a quick overview while he dressed.

"What do you think of the NFG's?" he asked.

"Hadn't met them yet. That's why I'm here getting you. I want us to meet them together."

Once he was dressed in dungarees, we headed to the galley. They were sitting at two different tables and I wondered why.

"You guys Clark and Baker?" I asked.

Clark, a black man was the Signalman and didn't seem particularly happy to be here. Baker was a skinny, red-headed kid that looked all of fifteen.

"I'm MM1 French and this is GM2 Fowler, except he only answers to 'Quacker'. I've been called a few different things but 'Iceman' seems to be the current one. Our last boat took an RPG hit and is out of commission. For now, we are being given the 866 until ours is repaired."

I went on to tell them about my conversation with the XO and told them everything I knew. I did leave out the part about Captain Willard. I found out that Clark was from Mississippi and had joined the Navy to get away from his home environment. He had been in-country for five months and had been on two boats that had been sunk by the VC. His best friend had died on the last boat.

Seaman Baker was from Indiana and had joined the Navy and was just a few weeks out of boot camp. He was totally green and he looked like he would jump out of his skin if someone yelled boo. I felt sorry for him but he would either toughen up or...well the options were limited.

We sat and talked for good half hour before others started to fill up the place. Just as I stood up, Ensign

Peterson came in, saw me standing there and walked over.

"Hey sailor, you stood me up," she said.

"Yeah right. I waited over and hour for you before I finally gave up and hit the rack."

"I know. I'm sorry about that. I got stuck in OR and couldn't get away. I feel really bad about standing you up."

"It wasn't like we were having a date. I guess I was just looking forward to talking to someone about anything but this stupid, senseless war."

"Why don't we do that now? Let's grab something to eat and head out to the fantail. We can talk there," she said.

"I can't think of anything I'd rather do. That would be excellent," I replied.

We grabbed some chow and carried our trays to the fantail. There were a couple of sailors just looking out at the water and we found a little area that was a bit more private.

"This should do," she declared and sat down holding her tray on her lap.

I joined her and we ate in silence for a few minutes. I was doing my best to not look at her legs stretched out and her skirt ridden up but it was sort of a losing battle.

"I guess you haven't seen a pair of legs in a while," she said.

I about swallowed my fork. Either she was a mind reader or she had seen me glancing over at her from time to time. I could feel my face turning red.

"Sorry. It has been awhile. I know I should be ashamed but damn, I'm not. I mean, that's one heck of a pair of gams. We don't see many where we are."

"It's okay. I understand. I hear stories about what it's like out there. I don't know how you guys do it. I mean, you face death daily. I could never do that," she said.

"What you do is pretty amazing. We get the hell blown out of us and you put us back together. A lot of guys would be dead if it wasn't for what you do here. I honestly don't see how you look at all this carnage day after day," I told her.

"Not the same thing. We have protection, beds, hot meals, and no one trying to kill us every second. Martin, you guys are some of the bravest people in the world."

"Martin? You looked up my name?"

"It's on your chart, remember?" she said.

"Yeah, I forgot about that. Out on the water they call me Iceman."

"Iceman? Why that name?"

"The crew gave me that. I guess because I tend to get into a zone and don't let anything bother me, no matter how bad it gets," I answered.

She looked at me for several moments before speaking, "So, you are cool under fire. Is that it?"

"Not cool, I just don't let it show. As captain, if I panic, everyone else will panic and that is a recipe for disaster," I explained.

She stood up and took my hand and pulled me up.

"Come on. I have a place we can go for a while."

"You don't own me anything."

"I know. This is what I want as well. Now come on," she said pulling me along.

CHAPTER TWENTY-FOUR

I was tired but happy when I got to the galley the following morning. The others were already eating when I walked in. Cracker took one look at me and gave me the peace symbol.

"Someone had a good night," he said.

"It was the extra sleep," I replied.

"Really? You must have moved to a different bunk. No one was in yours last night."

"I found other accommodations."

"No shit Sherlock," Cracker said and laughed.

After we finished breakfast, such as it was, we headed to the boat. When we got on deck, the chief was there checking over the rigging for the transport to Ben Koe. It was simply too far to go upriver without refueling several times and with the NVA still attacking it made sense to airlift it. The boat was attached to a CH47 Chinook Helicopter.

"The chopper will take you and your crew to your new duty station," the chief told us.

"When do we go?" I asked.

"Probably another twenty minutes. They are checking the sling and getting the Chinook ready to go."

"Okay, I need to attend to something. I'll be back in ten," I said and took off.

I went to the Sick Bay and found Ensign Peterson. Her eyes widened when she saw me and she slid over to where I was standing.

"Thought you were on your way out," she said.

"I am. I just wanted to say thank you for a most incredible night."

"It was just as incredible for me. I should thank you."

"Anyway. I just wanted to say goodbye."

"Thank you for that. Martin, please look after yourself. If you ever get back this way, please look me up."

"You can count on it," I said and turned and headed back to the boat.

The crew was getting ready to climb on the Chinook when I got back. The boat was secure and the engines were starting to turn over on the helicopter. Once we were in and seated, the pilot lifted the boat, we made a turn and headed up country.

Up here, everything looked green and peaceful. You couldn't tell people were doing their best to kill one other. Watching the foliage whisking by below us gave me a tranquil feeling and I could put the images of the war away for a while. At some point, I drifted off to sleep. I don't know how long I was out but I felt a change in altitude and the air was warmer.

I looked out and could see a large city. Looking closely, I could see flashes of mortars and howitzers spewing out fire. Obviously, the fighting was still raging in Saigon. It was hard to believe we hadn't pushed them out by this time.

On the repair ship, we were told battles were going on all up and down Vietnam. Kae Sanh was in a fight for their lives and a lot of our guys had been killed. I made me wonder what we were getting ourselves into.

It was late afternoon when we finally could see Ben Keo out of the chopper. They brought us in and set the boat in the water near a long pier. Once the boat was unhooked they sat the chopper down and we scrambled out. We immediately headed for the boat to check it over.

The initial inspection looked like everything had made it undamaged. I left the crew to make a more thorough check and I went to find the CP. After having to only ask twice I found the place and entered to report to Captain Willard.

"Machinist Mate First Class, Martin French reporting for duty," I told a Second Class, Personnel Man behind the desk.

He didn't look up but just held out his hand for my orders. It pissed me off and I wanted to smack him in the face. Instead of handing them to him, I tossed them on the desk. He looked up with a scowl but I just blew it off.

"You're with the boat they just brought in?"

"That would be correct."

"The Captain has been waiting for you to get here. They said it would be around noon and here it is going on," he said, glancing at his watch," almost 1400 hours."

I just shrugged. I don't fly the choppers. I got there when I got there. What the hell did they expect me to do about it?

The Personnel Man disappeared into the next room and then returned in just a couple of minutes.

"You can go in," he said.

When I went inside the Captain was seated behind an impressive desk. There was carpet on the floor and two stuffed chairs faced the desk.

"You're MM1 French?"

"Yes sir. Reporting as ordered."

"I read your after-action reports. Been in pretty good skirmishes. Took part in a couple of top-secret missions as well."

"Yes sir."

"We need men with experience. Three fourths of the boat captains are green horns. They make dumb mistakes that get the boats shot all to hell. We lost two yesterday, along with three KIA's and six WIA's. I'm hoping I can count on you to do a better job," he said.

"I'm not too keen on getting shot or having my boat blown out from under me so I will certainly do my best," I told him.

"They told me your boat was in top-notch condition. Reworked engines and the whole nine yards. Hopefully, that means we won't have to spend a lot of wasted time on repairs."

"They seemed pretty through at the tender. He went over everything they had done including a little extra armor around the cabin."

"Sounds good. Well, welcome aboard French. Report to Lieutenant Keeler. He will assign your patrol roster. You'll find him down at the docks. He will put you on the schedule and show you where you will be quartered."

"Lieutenant Keeler, aye, aye sir."

"Good luck to you and go kick some serious ass."

"Do my best," I replied.

I walked down to the small shed and found the Lieutenant holding a clip board and frowning.

"MM1 French reporting. I just left the Captain and he said I should come talk to you about the schedule and quarters for my men."

"I talked to a couple of your men. They said the boat had just been worked on at the tender."

"Actually, it is a loaner. Mine got its ass shot out of the water and is being re-built. They said the situation was critical here and I shouldn't wait for mine to be repaired."

"Oh, you could say that. We lose a boat every week it seems like. With yours, we will have a dozen serviceable boats to patrol. Right now, the VC are attacking anything that moves on the river. Ambushes are everywhere. You are really going to have your hands full here," the chief told me.

"We got caught with our pants down."

"Tet? Cease fire for New Years. What asshole thought they would keep their word? Probably that dumb ass Johnson. Him and his advisors. They couldn't plan a picnic without screwing it up."

I decided I would be better off not adding anything to the conversation. It wasn't that I disagreed, it just seemed prudent to keep my mouth shut.

"Okay, you will be going out at noon tomorrow. I'll introduce you to the other captain you will heading out with. His name is ET1 Ben Thornton. They call him 'Big Ben' on his ship. When I introduce you, you will understand."

We walked to the pier and started down it. I saw 'Big Ben' a few yards away. He towered over his crew. I guessing he was six-four and close to three hundred pounds. None of it looked like fat. The chief introduced us and we talked about some of the scrapes we had been through. For as big as he was, he had a nice calming voice. I met his crew and they were a lot like mine. Three seasoned vets and one NFG. We set a plan for out two crews to get together at evening chow.

The Lieutenant then took me to our hooches. They were a lot better than the last ones. They had wooden floors and lots of protection on the sides and top. Someone had put a lot of effort into securing them.

When we were done with that he gave me a quick tour of the base and went over some of the security procedures. It wasn't much different than back at Ving Long. When we were finished, he went back to whatever he had been working on and I went down and collected my crew.

I brought them back to the hooches and they went on about how much better they were. I brought them up to speed about the Captain and our meeting with Big Ben's crew at 1700 hours. After that we all went about squaring away our sleeping quarters. Quacker found a radio and flipped it on. The Armed Forces Vietnam Network was tuned in. The Doors were cranking out 'Hello, I love you' in the way only Jim Morrison can pound out.

We basically just hung out, goofing off. Baker was writing a letter to his High School sweetie. I decided to talk to Clark and find out more about him.

"Got time to talk?" I asked.

He just shrugged, so I took that as an invitation to proceed. I sat down on the floor across from him.

"So, where are you from?"

"Mobile, Alabama."

"You get drafted?"

"What do you think?" he said rolling his eyes.

"I have no idea. I'm guessing yes, from your reaction," I replied.

"This ain't my war, man."

"Why is that?" I asked.

"Ain't no reason for the brothers to die for a white man's war," he said.

"I see. Well Clark, let me tell you this, my man. On my boat, you will fight and give it a hundred and ten percent, or I will personally throw you ass overboard and you can tell the VC how you feel. A piss ass attitude don't mean shit to me. I have three 'white guys' that are putting their lives on the line to protect all of us, you included. You don't want to do that, get your ass off my boat," I told him and stood up.

"I just might do that," he snarled.

"That's fine. Just do it before we get underway. Go see Lieutenant Keeler and tell him I sent you to get transferred," I replied.

I was pretty worked up. This was my first experience with someone with a chip on their shoulder. What the hell did it matter who started this war? I thought about just going to talk to Keeler but decided that may be overreacting.

I walked all the way to the piers and back, trying to blow the steam but the longer I thought about it, the more upset I got. If I couldn't depend on him then he was a real detriment to the entire crew. He had been in country only a few more weeks than I had so what the hell was his problem? Was it a race thing? Maybe he didn't want to be on a crew with all white guys.

I decided when we met with Ben, I would take him aside and see what his thoughts were.

CHAPTER TWENTY-FIVE

It was amusing to watch the reaction of my men when they saw Ben for the first time. Cracker's eyes almost bugged out of his head. It was all I could do to keep from laughing.

He introduced us to his men and I did the same with mine. Clark was with us but I still wasn't sure about him. He was still sullen and it was starting to really piss me off. I thought about asking him if he wanted to swap boats and go with Ben, but decided I didn't want to put Ben on the spot like that. I would have to talk it over with him before I mentioned it to Clark.

After the introductions were over, we got down to the real reason for the meeting. We needed to have a plan of attack and I needed to be brought up to speed.

"We have section Z3 this time out," Ben said, unfolding a large map. The area of patrols was divided into four sections. Z1 through Z4. Our section, Z3 was from Bèn Kèo and ending at the bridge at Câu Gö Chi. It was a lot of river to cover with many potential ambush spots.

"I'll be lead boat since we have been up and down this sector a bunch of times. You follow fifty or so yards behind. We will stay in the center of the river. You never know where the gooks are going to pop out."

"Which side will you have your .50s trained on?"

"Good question. We will cover the port and you concentrate on the starboard. Keep your mic in your hand and shout out immediately if you see an RPG."

"Got it."

"It is due to start raining around the time we pull out. According to the weather people it is going to get heavy as the night goes on. Make sure everyone has their ponchos with them."

"Hear that guys?" I asked and they all nodded affirmative.

"We will concentrate most of our time close to the bridge. The gooks like to use it to smuggle men and weapons across. If you see something just open up. Don't wait for me. Fire first and we can talk it out later. I don't care if they look all innocent. Just mow their asses down."

"No problem," I replied.

"Good. We will meet at the boats at 1130 hours. That's what time the other boats will be returning. We need to debrief the Z3 guys and find out how it went and any potential hot spots. Once we are done we will get underway," Been told us.

"Right on," I said and immediately felt like a dumb ass. That's something some hippy would say.

My guys went down to the boat and made sure it was ship shape and that we had everything we needed. I picked up a set of maps of the area and sat on the stern of our boat and studied them, trying to visualize significant landmarks. I noticed a small village named Long Vĩnh. Geez, how did they ever keep all these places straight. I mean Our original base was Ving Long and now we were going to be going by a village with a similar name. I guess as Americans we don't always catch the nuances.

The map didn't really tell much about the bridge but I imagined it to be like so many others I had seen in Vietnam. Nothing more than a bunch of sticks lashed together with a handrail of some kind. How they scampered over them while carrying everything from bikes and weapons to bags of rice was beyond me.

I heard the returning boats before I saw them heading to the base. Ben waved and the boats nudged up against his.

"Hey Bro. You got a shit load of holes in your hull," he said taking off his sunglasses and looking the boat over.

"Got a little hot and heavy up at the bridge. Lots of slop heads moving goods. We shot the shit out of some of them but they got us in a crossfire and we had to break it off," the boat captain said.

"What kind of numbers are you talking about?"

"No idea. A shit load. VC and NVA mixed together. I'm going to talk to the LT about expanding the patrol area past the bridge. They know we are hanging out there. I think they have built some barges to ferry larger stuff across the river," the boat captain said.

Ben scratched behind his ear, deep in thought. It certainly made sense. They would sacrifice a few at the bridge if it meant that they could get more men and goods across the river a little further down river.

"I agree, it sounds like a good suggestion," Ben replied.

We shot the shit with the incoming crew and got to know them a little better. Their captain, Jimmy 'Jimbo' Parker was a MM1 the same as I was. We talked about where we had been and what ships we had served on.

They finally headed off to get some shut eye and we waited for Ben to return. It took a lot longer than I thought. Almost an hour went by before he returned.

"Sorry about the wait. We had to go to the Captain for his approval. Bottom line, he agrees it is worth giving it a shot. We can go until we hit 'bingo' fuel."

"Cool, let's boogie."

We fired up the boats and headed out. We still had to do our routine stops of the sampans if we came across any, but I knew Ben was anxious to test out this latest theory. I was excited about it as well. If we could catch them with their guard down, we could really score big.

As we rounded one bend a small village came into view. Evidently Ben had seen it many times before because I noticed there .50s were pointing in that direction. I had Quacker do the same thing with ours. Sure enough, just as Ben's boat drew even with the village, he started taking AK fire. Both of us opened up on the village.

Ben swung his boat around and pounded the village. I saw one of his men using the thumper to send shells into the village. We just followed his lead and continued the blow the hell out of the place. Two of the thatched roofs had caught on fire and smoke and flames were shooting high into the air.

Ben had his men continue to fire and shoot more grenades at the few standing huts left. He broke out a bow and arrow that he carried with him. It had some kind of material that he lit on fire and started shooting at the huts. Within minutes they were all ablaze. I guess he was tired of them taking pot shots at him so he just made sure the whole village was wiped out. He circled around and came up next to our boat.

"That should stop those damn gooks. They have pissed me off for the last time. The hell with this win the hearts and minds crap. Just blow their asses away and you don't have to worry about any of that bull," he said and roared off.

Well okay then. Not much I could say so I just headed out following behind him thirty yards or so. The water was like glass as we skimmed along. When the sun came up, we had to back down to keep from swamping the gooks in their sampans. Most of them looked like they were ready to sink at any moment.

We worked along the river for most of the morning, making routine stops. It seemed rather futile. All they had to do was wait for us to pass and head on down river and then sneak out with their cargo of whatever. It wasn't our job to question what we were supposed to be accomplishing. Yeah, we caught a few but I'm pretty sure a hell of a lot more got past us.

By late morning we were approaching the end of our patrol zone at the bridge.

"Ready to do this?" Ben asked.

"Lead on," was my reply.

We passed under the bridge, keeping a close eye on anyone above. We just drifted along, letting the current take us. We passed a few small villages but no one paid any attention to us. It wasn't until an hour or so later that it all changed. We came around a sharp bend and there it was. A makeshift bridge with hundreds of VC carrying supplies. Ben immediately had his men start firing and Cracker opened as well. We had caught them off guard for a few minutes which gave us a big advantage. We were blasting the hell out of them before they could even react.

They were falling in the water and on the bank as we lobbed everything we had at them. Baker was firing the thumper as fast as he could reload, sending men and materials flying in the air at each explosion. One of Ben's men was doing the same thing on the other bank. Once they started to react, we went into our usual defensive tactics. Ben took his boat right under the low hanging bridge and began blasting away from the other side. I made sure we weren't in his line of fire.

The crossfire was deadly. Ben's man went to work on the bridge with the thumper and after five or six shots the bridge collapsed. At least a hundred bodies were floating in the water. We had been lucky, other than a few holes in our boats, no one was seriously injured. The most serious injury was bullet ricochet that hit Clark on the cheek.

"Now that was some serious shit," Cracker said, not taking his eyes off the bank.

"Intense," Baker added.

"Far out," Cracker replied.

"I'm just glad no one got hit," I said.

"I got hit," Clark said, wiping the blood from his face.

"Naw. Hit's when your guts start oozing out of your body. You just got flesh wound," Cracker said.

Clark just gave him a dirty look but Cracker just smiled and went back to watching the shoreline in case they regrouped for a counterattack.

"I think we should go on down river a bit further," Ben said over the radio,

"Then let's do it," I agreed.

This time we cruised down rather than floating. Just about 10 klicks later everything went to hell. We spotted a second bridge but they must have known we were coming. They were set up and ready. They opened fire as soon as we were in range. You could see hundreds of muzzle flashes from the bridge and the shoreline. RPGs began peppering the water.

One RPG ricocheted of the top of Ben's boat. He was damn lucky. A few inches lower and he would have been ground beef. We were blasting away but we were far outnumbered. I heard Ben calling in the choppers for an air strike. All we could hope for was to hold on until we could get the choppers in the air and have them attack.

We reformed and started running in just enough to engage them and then drop back to safety. We wanted to keep them there until the gunships arrived to kick their asses. We did this for almost an hour before we saw the slicks come in over the treetops and open up on them. It was beautiful. They were absolutely cleaning their clock.

There were twice as many dead gooks in the water as the last time. It was a good day for our side. Once they had finished we decided it was time for us to head back to our routine patrol zone. Ben led the way with us following fifty yards behand.

The rest of the day was just the usual boring routine. Stopping boats and checking cargo. After the afternoon adventures this was a real let down. It was also a time to think about what you had just been through. Each guy handles it differently. Some it bothers, others like the rush, and some just see it as a job that needs to be done.

When we finished our patrol, Ben and I were summoned to the Captain's office. He wanted a personal account of what had happened. I guess he was already trying to find a way to take credit for all of this and make sure he got a medal. He kept asking about the body count. How many did you kill? Did you count them? He seemed very put out because we didn't take the time to do a head count. What an asshole.

CHAPTER TWENTY-SIX

Evidently Clark went to the Lieutenant and said he didn't want to be on PBR's any longer. He joined the Navy but not to fight in the jungles in a war that was started by the white men, not the brothers.

Now there is stupid and stupid. I guess because the Lieutenant was a black man he thought he could pull this off somehow. I don't know all the details but evidently the Lieutenant didn't take the news very well and had him brought up on dereliction of duty charges and he was court martialed. I guess being a brother didn't do him much good.

The war was strange. Here the President was telling people we had them on the run and yet Khe Sanh was still under attack and Saigon was not clear of the VC. We were being attacked more than ever before. The hit and run tactics were turning into sustained attacks. It was apparent to all of us in country that no one in Washington knew what they were doing. They were just reacting to events as they unfolded.

We could win this damn war if they would just let us. Let the people on the front lines determine the course of action. Bomb the hell out of North Vietnam until there was nothing left. Flatten Hanoi and this crap would be all over and we could all go home. Instead we were fighting their war and on their turf. Stupid. Of course, we couldn't say that to anyone but each other. So, we kept our mouths shut like good soldiers and sailors.

Our patrols now changed, based on our experience the last time out. The patrol zones were increased and we were to make exploratory patrols into previously uninvestigated tributaries. It was okay with us, it meant we didn't have to waste as much time stopping the local traffic.

I was short one man since Clark had been whisked off. We went out on our next patrol with just three on the crew which made me very nervous. As it turned out it was a very dull run and when we came back, the Lieutenant had our new replacement ready for us.

His name was Tim Taylor and we gave him the nickname of T squared all most immediately. He was an Electricians Mate Second Class and had been in country for four months. This was his first tour on PBR's. He had worked on a tender before this. He had volunteered for PBR's because he was bored on the repair ship.

"Where are you from Tim?" I asked him as we were all sitting on the stern of the boat.

"Montana. Butte, Montana. Big Sky country. God's gift to America," he said proudly.

"Pretty damn cold out there," Cracker chimed in.

"Naw. You get used to it. Just like here. Yeah, it's hotter than hell and humid here, but I've gotten used to it so it doesn't bother me much. Same with the cold," he said.

I've been here ten months and I sure the hell ain't used to it," Cracker responded.

"It's mind over matter. You just got to go with the flow," Tim replied.

"Right."

"Do you have any idea what you are getting into?" I asked.

"Not really, but I wanted to find out for myself. I've heard all the stories from the various crews that come to the tender for repair but some of it sounds kind of farfetched."

"Tim, Tim, Tim. I doubt if you have heard half of it. No matter what you heard it is a lot worse than you can ever imagine," I replied.

"I need to find out for myself," he said.

"Believe me, you will."

We weren't scheduled to go out again until midnight so I had the crew hit the rack or do whatever until we had our briefing at 2230. I decided on at least trying to cop some z's. I stripped down to just my skivvies and hit the rack. I tossed and turned for thirty minutes before I decided I wasn't going to get any real sleep inside our hooch. It was just too damn hot. I gathered my clothes and went back down to the boat and racked out. At least there was a slight breeze and the temperature was five or six degrees cooler. Thankfully, I was able to drift off. By now I had learned to grab some sleep even with the constant roar of artillery and jets zooming overhead. Between the gentle rocking of the boat and the dropping temperature as the sun started to go down I managed to get in some quality sleep time.

At 2230 we mustered with the Lieutenant for our briefing. It isn't exactly what we had expected.

"Okay listen up. We are going to extend the patrol area even further," he told us.

"Wait, LT We are already at the fuel window limit," Ben spoke up.

"We are going to have each boat load an extra 55-gallon drum of fuel to extend your range."

"You want us to refuel while underway with the possibility of getting caught right in an ambush?"

"Those are my orders. An extra tank of fuel has already been loaded on the boats going out at 2400 hours. When you hit bingo fuel you are to refuel and go another thirty klicks before turning back," he said.

From the moaning and groaning it was apparent none of the boat captains were very happy with this latest development. I had been through the refueling while underway twice before and while it was difficult and time consuming, it wasn't impossible to do. Getting the drums in position was the hardest part while the boat was moving.

The discourse fell on deaf ears. We had our orders and there wasn't a heck of a lot we could do about it. When we were dismissed and walking back to the boats, Ben stopped me.

"This is some Mickey Mouse bullshit. What do you think about just going on our usual patrol and forgetting the refueling crap?" he asked.

"There is some risk to that. If just one of our crew members bragged to one of the other crews we would find our butts in some pretty hot water," I answered.

"None of my people would say anything."

"And you're sure a hundred percent?"

"Pretty sure," Ben said.

"Look, you're the lead boat. I'll do whatever you do. If you go on, I'll be right behind you. If you stop and dump the fuel overboard, we will do the same. I don't know two of my people very well but that is the chance we will have to take if we decide to not continue on," I replied.

"Crap. This totally sucks. This sounds like something the dumb ass Captain thought up."

"I guess it doesn't really matter. All you have to do is decide what action you are going to take.," I said.

"Shit," he said shaking his head and walking to his boat.

I understood exactly where he was coming from. He was caught between a rock and a hard place. His decision would affect all eight of us. I'm glad I didn't have to make the call.

At 2400 we left base and headed down stream. I could almost hear the gears in Ben's brain turning, trying to decide the best course of action.

One thing for sure, we didn't have to wait long before we ran into a VC ambush. We were just motoring along when both of us found ourselves taking fire from the shoreline. They must have waited until they were sure we were in the kill zone before opening up. Cracker was the first to react, he opened up immediately, followed by everyone else. Two RPG's come streaking out from the bank and just missed Ben's boat by a few yards. Cracker opened up on that spot and he must have gotten them because that was the last grenade from that area.

We both swung our boats around and took another run at them, blasting the shoreline with everything we had. Baker was using the thumper once again almost non-stop. On the third pass the fire from the shore dwindled to just sporadic AK fire.

Either they had fallen back or we had done a pretty good number on them.

We made one last pass but no one fired at either boat so we continued down river. We had never received gun fire from this area and it had caught both of us off guard. It was a reminder that you couldn't let your guard down for even a minute. The second you do; it all goes to hell. We made it to the bridge with no further ambushes. Tension was already running high so when we went under it and headed further downstream, it took another jump.

Sure enough, the makeshift bridge we had destroyed before had been repaired and we started taking fire. This time we were all ready and just trashed the bridge from one end to the other. We could see the bodies falling off the bridge and into the water. One RPG came streaking down but missed by a wide margin.

We concentrated our fire until we managed to destroy the bridge again. I was thinking that it was probably an exercise in futility. The VC would probably start rebuilding it as soon as we left the area. We were now at the point where Ben had a decision to make. Either we turned back, dumped the extra fuel or we went on until it was time to refuel.

"What are we doing?" I asked Ben over the radio.

"What would you do?"

"Man, you make the call. I'll support whatever you decide."

"That ain't what I asked. What would *you* do?"

"Go on," I finally replied.

"Yeah. I figured. Okay, but this is uncharted area for us so you guys reload everything and be ready."

"Don't worry about that. I can guarantee we are ready. You want to keep the separation of the boats the same or tighter?" I asked.

"Let's maintain thirty yards or so."

"Okay Ben. We have your six," I replied.

"Knew you would. Alright, here we go," he said and off we went further down the river than any time in the past.

CHAPTER TWENTY-SEVEN

We had gone maybe ten klicks down river when another makeshift bridge came into view. Immediately we opened fire. Just as fast, Charlie unloaded on us. They must have set up strong points because the volume of fire was intense.

We broke into our attack formation and began systematically attacking both the bridge and the shoreline. While we didn't have the advantage of superior fire power, we did have speed and maneuverability. RPG's were splashing all around both of our boats. I don't know how many were being fired but it seemed like every thirty seconds one would land near us.

Suddenly, Ben's boat almost leaped out of the water as an PRG hit someplace near the cabin. A huge fireball erupted and the boat went dead in the water. Two more RPG's slammed into the boat, ripping it in two pieces. The front was pointing straight up and within seconds the stern disappeared under water. We continued to fire at the bridge as I headed to the stricken boat. I called in a sit-rep while maneuvering toward Ben's boat.

Taylor was using the field glasses to see if he could locate any of Ben's crew members. It's hard at night while trying to avoid getting your ass shot off. Bullets ripped into the side of our boat and I saw Taylor just standing there. His body was up right but his head was missing. He crumpled to the floor.

"Over there," Baker shouted, pointing.

I wheeled the boat over and headed to a body floating in the water. I backed the boat down and Clark reached over to grab it. He could get ahold of it but couldn't pull it on board.

"Hold on to him. We are going to try to get out of range," I shouted.

I spun the wheel and just then a grenade slammed into the side of the boat. I saw Clark flipping in the air, head over heels and landing hard in the water. We had lost power as well. Neither engine was working.

"Come on Cracker, we have to go." I yelled.

I got ready to jump overboard but saw that Cracker was still in the turret. I ran over and saw he was bleeding from a bullet hole in his right arm. I used my legs and arms to get him out of the turret. Just then another RPG hit the nose of the boat. It threw both of us to the deck. AK fire was peppering the boat from bow to stern as I drug him over to the side and shoved him into the water. I had just slid over the side when another grenade smashed into the side of our boat.

I grabbed Cracker around his life vest and started swimming toward the closest shoreline which was just a few yards away. Once I got there I tied Cracker's vest to a low hanging tree branch and took mine off and tied it off as well. I went under water and started trying to make my way back to where I had last seen Baker.

I had to stick my head up a couple of times to get orientated and to see if I could locate him. Luckily, the gooks were more concerned about the boat and kept riddling it with machine gun fire. I was just about to give up when I saw a head bobbing up and down in the water a few yards from me. I dove down and swam until I thought I was close. I surfaced just a few feet from Baker, grabbed hold of his vest, and started pulling him toward where I had left Cracker. I was lucky again since no one seemed to have spotted me. If it has been daylight I would never have made it.

When I got over to Cracker I checked Baker out. He was out of it but he had a good pulse. I took the time to check Cracker as well. The hole in his arm was bigger than a bullet wound I discovered. I could see a piece of shrapnel sticking out of it. That was going to make it more difficult. I had intended to stuff something into the hole to stem the flow of blood but there was no way I was going to remove the shrapnel. I used my knife to cut the sleeve off my shirt and folded it up and made a makeshift bandage. I used the other sleeve to make a wrap to hold it in place as best I could.

I kept to the tree line next to the bank under a bunch of branches that were an overhang. I could hear Charlie searching along the banks and wondered when they would discover us. All I had was my .45 Colt but I was determined I would not be taken alive. I would shoot as many of them as possible before they killed me.

I sneaked a glance at my watch and was surprised to find it was 03:45 I would have sworn it was much later. They searched for another hour before then finally gave up. I waited another thirty minutes before I decided to risk trying to move the three of us upriver. I had a few things going for me. One was that the VC usually disappeared during the day light hours, kind of like bats. Second, the current was relatively mild along the shoreline. Third, was the fact that the shoreline was covered right down to the river in most places. On top of that, I had only seen a few villages along this section of the river. Last of all, I was hoping that once the base realized we were overdue they would send out a patrol to look for us.

For now, all we had to do was not get discovered as I tried to maneuver us upstream. This area was far too active with VC to stay in place. It would only take one person looking where we happened to be hiding and it would be all over.

I tied Cracker to Baker and then tied them both to my jacket. I would pull us along from one tree branch to another stopping often to listen for any voices. One thing that did bother me was that the misquotes were having a feast on me. I would swat ten away and twenty more would take their place. I knew Cracker and Baker were being eaten alive but there wasn't anything I could do about it.

By 0500 we had gone two or three miles by my estimate. My arms were getting tired from reaching up constantly but the more distance I put between them and us the better.

I had stopped to rest and check on Cracker and Baker when a firefight broke out just a few hundred yards from the river. Obviously, our people were in contact. You can always tell the AK's from the AR by the rate of fire and difference in sound. It was also easy to tell that our guys were heavily outnumbered. I would have loved to found a way to contact them and let them know our position, but not only was it impractical, it was impossible.

Finally, the gun fire slowed and then stopped. I don't know who broke off the assault but if I had to guess I would say our side did. There were just too many of them.

The sun finally broke over the treetops and another day in beautiful Vietnam began. Let the killing commence. As I worked my way upriver as best I could I thought about how stupid fighting a war this way was. Even what we were doing on the river was half-assed. We sneak around, they ambush us, we blow the hell out of them and then a few miles later it all plays out again.

A good example is the last fire fight. We probably killed close to a hundred VC and they killed five of our guys. We shot the hell out of the bridge but by tomorrow it would be right back in place and either I, or someone else, would do it all over again. Other than the loss of lives, what was really gained? Surely someone would recognize the futility of having a bunch of guys running around killing each other with no real objective in mind.

With the sunup, the activity of the VC pretty much came to a halt. Periodically, I could see a few villagers come down to the river but none of them were carrying guns. Even so, I made sure we were well hidden in case they ran off to get a soldier. That meant occasionally I would have to hang on to an overhead branch for fifteen or twenty minutes. It was difficult to hang on to my guys and the branches at the same time but I had no other option.

Everything would have been so much simpler if all we had to do was float down the river but such was not the case. I kept thanking the good Lord that the current wasn't bad. By 0800 I estimated we were 4 miles from where we had started. I kept stopping and checking on my two guys. It really bothered me that neither of them had woken up since I pulled them to the shore. Cracker was still breathing but it had become more ragged.

I finally found a place where I could get up on the shore and pull them up as well. It was no easy task and I was afraid I was making too much noise. I finally managed to get them laid out. We had all been in the water a long time and even though the river isn't all that cold, I was still starting to get chilled from hypothermia. While we were all laying there, I took my .45 apart and cleaned it the best I could. The things are pretty indestructible but I wanted to take care of it. It was all I had for defense.

As the sun moved higher in the sky, a few beams of sunlight filtered through the canopy. I moved Cracker and Baker so as much sunlight as possible fell on them. I figured it would do them some good. After lying on the bank for a couple of hours, I decided we had pressed our luck as about as much as we dared. I wasn't all that fond of getting back in the water but we needed to keep moving.

It took as much effort to drag them back into the water as it did to get them out. Once we were in, I started tediously pulling them up stream again. I was only able to continue for an hour before I just couldn't pull us along any further. I needed to find a safe place to rest and build my strength up. Unfortunately, it was almost a half an hour later before I found a spot I thought was safe enough for me to get them out of the water and grab a quick nap.

It was 10:30 by the time I got Baker and Cracker up on the shore and laid out. I dragged myself out and lay there just resting. Getting cover for the three of us was critical so I cut some branches and placed them over the two men. When I was satisfied with their coverage I made a place for me to lie down.

I was bone tired but even so, it took some time before I finally drifted off.

CHAPTER TWENTY-EIGHT

The sound of automatic gunfire startled me awake. I peered out between the tree branches and saw one of our boats firing at the shoreline just across from us. From the looks of the battle, the two boats were up against a large contingent of NVA rather than the usual VC. The fire power was considerably more pronounced than usual.

Even from where I sat, I could see the PBR's getting blasted as bit and pieces were being blown off them. Finally, the two boats turned and headed back upriver. I looked at my watch, I was shocked to see it was 16:20 hours. I had slept almost six hours. The boats must have been looking for us since we didn't return at our scheduled time.

I heard choppers coming from upriver and they were going to kick the hell out of the NVA, but they flew right on over, heading to some other destination. It was a big letdown, but there was nothing that could be done about it.

Checking on my crew, I found that Baker had his eyes open but didn't seem to be coherent. I couldn't get him to speak or even nod that he understood who I was. Even though he hadn't recognized me, I felt better about his condition. Time was what he probably needed to heal.

Cracker was still losing a small amount of blood but his heartbeat was stronger and I had hopes that he would make it as well. The bad news was that we needed to get moving again. We had spent more time here that I would have liked. Added to that was the fact that none of us had eaten in several hours and there was no potable water to drink.

We may have been surrounded by water but the Mekong Delta was basically a cesspool. Human waste, animal waste, industrial runoff, Agent Orange, and all kinds of chemicals were present. Even most of the Vietnamese didn't drink the water. This was a real problem that we were facing. We could go without food for a while but we needed water. The problem was how to go about getting an adequate amount for the three of us.

It's funny how your mind works. Once I started thinking about water it seemed like that was the only thing I could focus on. Even the misquotes seemed less of a problem. My mouth became dryer and while I tried to concentrate on getting from one branch to the next, water kept creeping into my mind. If I was needing water, it meant my crew probably needed it even more. I knew I was going to have to find a source.

Pulling along from branch to branch was a slow process and my arms were getting tired again. No matter how I arranged Cracker and Baker, it was difficult to hold on to the branches and keep them in tow. We had been at it for almost an hour before we came to an open area. The trees ended and the next crop was a good thirty or forty yards away.

This was not good. A large rock was at the edge of the bank and I could see a basket setting nearby. Leaning out I could just see the very top of a hut. Either I was on the edge of a village or some farmer lived there. Either way it was a real dilemma. Tying the two men off to a branch I decided to check out the area as much as possible without getting my ass shot off.

On my stomach, I crawled slowly up the incline, stopping to listen every few feet. I could see more of the thatched roof of the hut but so far hadn't heard a sound. At the top of the incline I quickly raised my head. I didn't see anyone around so I took another peek, longer this time, trying to get a lay of the land. There was just the one hut and two paths. One leading down to the river and one away from the place. I also saw what looked like a small well and a bucket.

I figured that the place was probably abandoned. If it was, I could get the men out of the water and let them dry out. I decided to lie there for several minutes and just listen. We had come too far to risk everything on a safe place to dry out. I waited almost ten minutes before I stood up, crouched over, and got a good look around.

Nothing. There was no fire, no animals, and no other person around that I could see. I slowly made my way to the hut and poked my head inside. Nothing but a large woven bowl and a small stove that was used for cooking. I went over to the stove and felt the ashes. They were stone cold. I felt a lot better about the situation. The next thing I checked out was the well. I lowered the bucket but it was apparent that it was empty. That was probably what caused whoever lived here previously, to abandon the hut in the first place.

Making my way back to the river, I pulled the two men out of the Delta and up on the shore. Once they were untethered I carried first Cracker up to the hut and then Baker. I'm not sure it was an improvement or not, but Baker was starting to mumble a few words. It was impossible to make out what he was saying but at least he was talking again.

Once they were both inside, I stripped all their clothes off except their skivvies and wring them out. I dropped my clothes as well and took them all outside to dry in the sun. Finished with that, I went in the hut and stretched out. I was absolutely bushed and fell asleep with my gun in my hand.

I was a startled when I awoke. The sun was setting and the hut was dark. I looked over and checked on the men. They both had their eyes closed and when I touched Baker to check his pulse, his eyes opened.

"Where are we?" he asked.

I jumped back. I wasn't expecting him to be coherent.

"Some place along the Delta. Our boat got blown out from under us. I was able to get you and Cracker to shore. I've been trying to work our way upriver. Right now, we are in an abandoned hut trying to recuperate before going on. How are you feeling?"

"Weird. I don't remember hardly anything. What about the rest of the guys?"

"Gone. Same for the other boat. Either they were ready for us or we ran into a hell of a lot bigger force."

"And I've been out since then?" he asked.

"Yeah. Cracker has too. He has a sizable piece of shrapnel in his arm. It isn't bleeding as bad as it was but he needs medical attention or he isn't going to make it."

"And no one has come looking for us?" he said.

I told him about the two PBR's that had been coming down river when the NVA opened up on them.

"So, we have to get back on our own. That's just swell," he said bitterly.

"We could be floating out into the South China Sea face down. All things considered, I would rather be trying to make it back," I replied.

"What about slicks?"

"I saw two fly over, but they weren't look for us from what I could tell."

"You don't happen to have any food or water, do you?" he asked.

"Sorry. The well outside is dry and there is nothing to eat," I explained.

We sat in silence for quite a while. I'm sure Baker was trying to process what had happened. I could see him shake his head a couple of times.

"Alright, what is the plan?" Baker asked after a few moments.

"We are going to have to slip back into the water. At least I have you to help with Cracker. We will just keep moving upriver. Hopefully, they will send another search party out for us and we can flag it down."

"I hate to mention this, but what happened to our clothes?" he asked, looking around.

"Ah. I set them in the sun to dry out," I replied going out to get them.

I brought them back and we dressed and then got Cracker dressed as best we could. It would be so much easier if he was awake, but there was nothing we could do about it right now. I hefted him over my shoulder and carried him back down to the river.

"I know you feel better now, but I want you to tie yourself on to me. Cracker will be tethered to you. We work our way slowly up the river by grabbing overhead branches and pulling us along," I explained after we were back in the water.

I had Baker make sure Cracker's head was out of the water before we started off once again. I was disappointed to some extent. The going was only marginally easier. Baker was pretty weak and his arms gave out after only a half hour. We continued, taking a break whenever my arms got too tired to pull us along. The breaks were becoming more frequent.

The night was consuming the day and it made progress even harder. We also had to stop and listen from time to time. Voices would come drifting from either across the water or on our side. The VC were on the prowl. By 0300 we needed to get out of the water. Baker was shivering uncontrollably and I was really worried about Cracker. It was another twenty minutes before we found a place to drag ashore. I didn't like it much but with the dark, I figured it would do for a few hours.

We had no more than settled down when we heard a lot of Vietnamese voices just a few yards from where we were huddled together for warmth. I could smell the nasty smoke from their cigarettes and hear them laughing and mentioning 'Running Dogs' which was a term used for American GI's. They were relieving themselves in the river and had all sat down, taking a break.

I had my .45 ready, but in reality, there was little I could do against a bunch of VC with automatic weapons. All we could do at present was to wait them out and hope they didn't decide to stay there all night. An hour went by and they didn't seem like they were thinking about moving anytime soon. The space was just too open at that point to get from one set of branches to the other without someone spotting us, even in the dark.

Baker was starting to shiver again and I wondered how long he could hold out. Automatic gun fire erupted nearby and the VC jumped up and started in the direction it was coming from. Once they were all gone, we made a hurried dash for the next set of branches, not worrying about the noise we were making. We reached the other side without incident and continued to put distance between them and us.

At this point I had no idea how far we had come or how far we had to go for that matter. We hadn't reached the limit of our normal patrol because I hadn't seen the bridge yet. I decided I couldn't think about how far we had to go, but to concentrate on how far we had managed to come without being discovered.

The biggest things we were facing, besides Charlie, was lack of water, food, and a place to dry out and rest. We needed to obtain all of those to keep our strength up.

CHAPTER TWENTY-NINE

Ben Keo was not presently worried about what had happened to the two boats. They were in their own fight for survival. By-passed in the earlier Tet Offensive, they were now under heavy attack by a determined force with devastating fire power.

Mortars had obviously been preregistered because they hit the CP that housed Captain Willard. Everyone was occupied with trying to keep the camp from being overrun but no matter how many they killed, more kept on coming.

Sappers were able to breech the outer barbed wire before being repelled by M60 machine gun fire. The VC were using heavy machine guns and mortars along with wave after wave of men with AK's. Captain Willard was shaken but not seriously hurt.

"I want a sit rep," he yelled into the phone.

"Sir. I'm a bit busy at the moment," Lieutenant Keeler replied.

"I need to know what's going on."

"Captain, we are getting the shit kicked out of us. The additional slicks are still twelve minutes out. They have two Phantoms on the way in but they are at least eight minutes from target. No fire base can support us now. They have other priority targets."

"Can we hold on until the fast movers get here?"

"I don't see we have a choice. We are holding our own at the moment but I think they are just regrouping to make another assault," Keeler told him.

"Any causalities?"

"I don't have a count of KIA or WIA."

"What about the VC? Got a body count?"

"Sir, that is impossible at this time. I'm sure the hell not going out to count dead gooks."

"Alright, but as soon as possible I want a body count."

"Copy that."

When he was finished with the Captain he turned to the Chief, "Can you believe that moron wants a body count?"

"Oh, I can believe it alright. It seems everything is centered around who has the highest body count. Hell, everyone adds a few extra to the count if they have any brains. He figures if he gets a high enough one, it could lead to a promotion. It's a hell of a way to fight a war," the Chief replied.

"While we are in kind of a lull, could you have someone find out the condition of our men and get them more ammo. And one more thing, get some water to the men."

"On it," he said.

Keeler started doing an inventory of the damage inflicted so far. The pier was almost destroyed as well as the repair shop. Three PBR's had taken direct mortar hits and had burned to the waterline. Four others were badly damaged. The other three looked like they wouldn't need much to put them back in commission.

By the time he was finished surveying the area, the Chief had returned.

"I sent Morris to check on the men. We have six KIA," he said handing Keeler the dog tags from the dead sailors.

"Geez. I suppose the wounded is a lot worse."

The Chief replied, "Indeed it is. Eighteen wounded. Six of those seriously enough that we need to medavac them immediately. The medics are doing all they can but one man lost his arm and another most of his leg."

"I'll...."

A mortar exploded a few yards from them. The shock wave threw them to the ground like they were rag dolls. AK fire erupted as the VC started their second attack. Their timing was bad. They were out in the open when the two Phantoms came streaking over the treetops and let loose with their tanks loaded with napalm. They were right on target as the red-orange fire ball and black smoke engulfed at least half of the men.

The men closest to the wire had no place to go. If they tried to go back, they would have to run directly into the flames. They were caught in no-man's land and became easy targets for the sailors defending the base.

Just minutes later the two slicks arrived and began to blast the remaining VC and the area that they had been staging in. It was going to be a slaughter. The sailors stood and cheered as the gunships continued to mow the rest of Uncle Charlie's men into little more than blood and guts.

The back of the attack had been broken and now the process of cleaning up and getting the base operational again became the primary concern. The effectiveness of the PBR patrols had essentially been stopped. With only a few undamaged boats even available, they were fundamentally out of commission until they could get the piers repaired and the remaining floating boats repaired.

Captain Willard was still screaming for a body count. He didn't even ask about how many sailors had been killed or wounded. As it turned out nine were now listed as KIA and twenty-two WIA. A dust-off was called in for the most seriously wounded.

Lieutenant Keeler was just about at the boiling point after the Captain called for the fourth time to ask about a body count. He finally had someone make an estimated count without leaving the complex. There was no way he was going to ask someone to go out and count dead gooks.

When the Captain called for a fifth-time, Keeler told him that it was almost impossible to tell because of the napalm strike but the best estimate was around two hundred. The Captain was insistent that the count was higher than that and he wanted the Lieutenant to send out a patrol and physically count the bodies.

Keeler waited an hour before telling the Captain that the physical count had determined there were two-hundred and ninety-seven bodies. This seemed to make the Captain happier although he was insistent that there had to be more. Rather than argue with the Captain, Keeler said it was possible that the count could be higher because of various body parts that could have been a VC. That seemed to please the Captain and he said he would report that three-hundred and twenty had been killed and several hundred others wounded.

The Lieutenant said it sounded about right. He wasn't going to fight a losing battle. If the Captain wanted to jack up the body count, it was no skin off his nose. The Chief just shook his head when Keeler related the story. It was so typical of how the game was being played. The officer in charge that had the largest body count got the glory and the medals to prove how gallant they were.

It seemed to pacify the leaders back home as well. The White House could go on television and tell the American people how well the war was going and that it wouldn't be long before we could bring our boys back home. Of course, few believed the rhetoric, but it was the official version being played to the American audience. The opposition to the Vietnam War was increasing back in the US. Even though Tet had been a dismal military failure, it had accomplished a far greater victory in the political and media arena.

All Lieutenant Keeler and the men on the ground knew was that Charlie was nowhere close to giving up on the war. If anything, they were more determined than ever to drive the Americans out of their country.

CHAPTER THIRTY

Having no idea what was going on at Ben Keo, I continued to hold out hope that a patrol boat would come along and rescue us. We had been in the water for forty-eight hours and had nothing to drink or eat. Both men were getting weaker. Baker had stopped talking again and his head was lolling from side to side as I pulled us all along. I knew time was running out for both men.

I gave a thought of just trying to hide them and heading off to the base alone to get help but leaving them didn't seem like such a great idea. I decided it would be better to keep going.

At 14:30 hours I found another flattened area leading down to the river. Obviously, it had been used a great deal. The path was quite pronounced. Like the last place we had found, no one seemed to be around. I could see four huts by lifting up on my toes as far as possible. A well was located near the second hut. If it wasn't empty like the previous one, it would go a long way towards increasing our chances of survival.

I once again tied off Baker and Cracker and slowly made my way up the path until I could duck walk to the first hut. I quickly peeked in but saw nothing of significance. No one was in the hut and it appeared to have been abandoned. I slipped around to the back to get a look at the other huts. From what I could see, it looked like the small village was uninhibited, just like the last place I had found earlier.

Once again, I had a decision to make that would affect all three of us. Either I checked out the entire cluster of huts or abandoned the idea and slipped back into the water. I wrestled with the decision while leaning against the closest hut to the river. The sun felt good and I knew both the other men needed to get out of the water. I made my decision.

I climbed through the window and dropped down waiting for someone to shout out but nothing happened. I quickly glanced over at the next hut but saw nothing suspicious. I made sure I had a round in the chamber of my .45. Sneaking around from place to place wasn't going to help all that much. Either there were VC or no one was here any longer.

I walked to the next hut and checked inside. Nothing. It was the same with the third and fourth. I found no VC but I found a bonanza in one hut. There was an area that was used for cooking. A traditional rice cooking pot and a small stove were in one corner. I rummaged around and found three or four large hands full of rice. All I needed was water and I could get some nourishment into all of us. Water. We needed water in the worst way. I ran out to the well and looked down. It was dark and I couldn't tell if it held water or not. If it was like the last place, we would be in the same predicament.

I found a small pebble and dropped in the well. I heard it hit the water below. I was so relieved my knees almost buckled. I needed to get the men out of the water and let them start drying out. It took a lot of energy to finally half-pull, half-carry them up to the huts and lay them out in the sun. Once that was finished, the next task was to get some water.

I found the bucket attached to a rope and lowered it into the well. Cranking the handle to raise it told me that I had hit the jackpot. There was no ladle but that didn't matter. I poured it into my mouth directly from the bucket. It was one of the most wonderful things I had ever tasted. I gulped down big mouthfuls before I carried it over to where Cracker and Backer lay.

I gently picked up Cracker's head, parted his lips and poured a little water into it. He didn't react. The water just ran down the sides of his mouth. He was in serious trouble and unless I could get him to eat and drink I knew he wouldn't make it. I tried twice more but he was not swallowing. As much as I hated to, I moved over to Baker. I raised his head and poured a small amount of water in his mouth. His lips moved and he swallowed the water. I did it again and he let it slide down his throat and his eyes fluttered. I gave him two more sips and then laid his head down. He moaned and mumbled something that I couldn't make out.

Food. They needed food and that was going to take time. First wood had to be gathered, water fetched for the pot, and then cooking it. The water and wood weren't much of a concern but starting the fire, well that would be the real challenge. Being a non-smoker, I had no way to start a fire. I ran over and checked Baker and he had a Zippo Lighter but I seriously doubted it would work after spending so much time in the water. Fortunately, Cracker had a cheap-o Bic which was more likely to work. I tested the Bic and it lit on the second try. I now had everything I needed. It only took a few minutes to gather the wood I need and to get the water.

I knew there was a real risk of starting a fire. It could easily attract the VC or even our own troops could open up on us not knowing we were Americans. Regardless of the danger, it was one I was willing to take.

Once the water started to boil I added the rice and let it simmer for several minutes before putting my helmet over the pot. I rotated between checking on the men and watching the rice. Luckily, I still had my fork and spoon with me. I checked a few morsels every once in a while, until it was done. Using my shirt tail, I took the rice out to the men and sat down. I decided to start with Baker since he had been the most responsive. Lifting his head, I placed a fork full of rice in his mouth. I slapped his face.

"Chew Baker. We have food. You need to eat," I said to him.

He moaned but slowly chewed the rice. I gave him a second bite and he managed this one better. Alternating rice with a sip of water seemed the best way to get the food down. His eyes fluttered several times and then he opened them.

"Iceman?"

"Hey Baker, welcome back to the land of the living."

"Man, I don't feel like I am very much alive," he said.

I placed another fork full of rice in front of him and he downed it immediately.

"Where are we?" he asked looking around.

"I'm not exactly sure. I figure we are getting close to the bridge that was our original patrol boundary."

"No one has come looking for us still?"

"Not that I am aware of. I fell asleep a few times but I think a boat would have awaken me," I said.

"So, you have been just tugging the two of us along?"

"I sure wasn't about to leave you. The VC were crawling all over the place. They would have probably found you at some point."

"How about Cracker?" Baker asked.

"Not good. I can't get him to eat or even drink. If we don't get him medical attention soon, he isn't going to make it."

"Geez. They knew we were coming, didn't they?" Baker asked.

"Seemed that way to me. We got our asses handed to us. Yeah, they knew we were coming."

"What a frickin' SNAFU."

"You could certainly say that," I agreed.

"So, what is the plan now?"

"We are going to hole up here while the sun is still up. I want to try to get Cracker to eat and drink, at least something. At sunset, we will get back into the water and continue to try to make our way up stream."

"That's a long way," Baker lamented.

"It's the only option that I see at this point unless we want to just hang out here and hope they send a patrol boat looking for us," I replied.

He didn't say anything. He just closed his eyes and leaned his head on the hut, letting the warm sun wash over him. I worked on Cracker, trying to get him to eat or drink something. I managed to get a little water down this throat but that was about all. His pulse was very week and I wondered if he had internal injuries as well. His skin was almost a ghostly white.

At some point, I had to go to relieve myself. I walked a few yards away and bent down to take care of business. I was on the far side of the hut. When I finished, I pulled up my pants and headed back. I stopped dead in my tracks. I could hear shouting in Vietnamese. I only knew a few basic words but there was no mistaking 'Giơ tay Lên'. Hands up. I could hear Baker trying to talk to them and keep them calm but they were getting pretty worked up.

Another voice said 'bắn chúng' which meant shoot them. The two VC started arguing about whether to shoot them or take them back for interrogation. I guess one of the guys wanting to take them back because he shouted Đứng lên which I was pretty sure meant stand up. I could only think of three options. Wait and follow them and look for an opportune time to jump them. Two, I could just let the VC take them and just strike out on my own, or three, step around the coroner and hope my .45 worked and shoot them both. It really wasn't that much of a choice.

I could hear Baker trying to explain why Cracker wasn't getting up but they were just getting angrier. It was time to move.

CHAPTER THIRTY-ONE

I checked to make sure I had a shell in the chamber and sprang around the corner. I fired, BAM, I could see the closest VC get bowled over backwards. The second one was raising his AK when I shot. BAM, BAM. The first shot missed him but the second one caught him in the throat. His eyes went wide and blood spurted out of his neck. He was still holding the AK so I shot him in the chest and he fell backwards. Silence followed as both Baker and I took in what had just happened.

"Geez," Baker said, "I thought we were goners."

"What? You thought I would just leave you?" I asked.

"The thought entered my mind. You didn't even know if your gun worked. You could have gotten your ass shot off."

I walked over and looked at the two men I had just killed. They were boys really. I figure they were between thirteen and fifteen. I wondered how long they had been fighting this stupid war. It is one thing to kill from a distance when you are out on the water and firing at the shoreline. You don't really know if you actually killed someone or not. I suppose it was like that for most of the grunts out in the boonies.

Baker had been right about one thing. I really had no way of knowing if my gun would fire or not. I just reacted to the situation. I could have gotten all three of us killed if the .45 had failed.

Baker broke me out of my trance, "Is there any more rice or water?"

"Lots of water but only a little rice left. Let me see if I can get something down Cracker first and then we can split what is left."

"You're wasting your time with Cracker. No way is he going to be able to eat, or drink for that matter. He is too far gone," Baker said.

I just ignored him and went about trying to get a small amount of food down his mouth. I placed a small portion in his mouth and moved his jaw. When it was chewed as best as I could do, I rubbed his throat, trying to make him swallow. It was useless. Trying the water yielded the same results. Nothing I could do was going to make him eat or drink.

I laid his head down and took turns with Baker eating small mouthfuls of the rice. We washed it down with more water from the well.

"What about the VC?" Baker asked.

"I'll pull them into one of the huts before we take off which we need to do in less than an hour."

We sat, letting the remaining rays of sunlight warm our bodies and faces. Finally, it was time to go. Baker and I dragged the two dead VC bodies into the closest hut. Once we were done with that, I drew one last bucket of water and we drank our fill. Cracker had a canteen on him so we filled it to take with us.

I picked up the 2 AK – 47's and checked the magazines. There were fully loaded clips, which gave us sixty rounds total. I gave one of the AK's to Baker and slung the other one over my shoulder.

I took Cracker's right side and Baker took his left and we virtually dragged him down to the water. Before we left I took the magazine out of the AK and made a head scarf out of my pant leg. I secured it in the head band to keep it out of the water as much as possible. I had Baker do the same thing. It would take a little longer to load the AK but at least the ammo would be dry.

Once we were back in the water, I attached us to each other with me in the lead, Cracker in the saddle, and Baker as rear end Charlie. I felt pretty good overall. I had some food in my stomach, plenty of water to quench my thrust. The first hour went amazingly well. We were able to make good progress until we came to the area of the bridge that used to serve as out patrol boarder.

We could see a lot of activity even at this time of night. People with carts loaded with animals, rice, and other crops were heading in one direction. People going the other way were either empty handed or only had small baskets full of food. Every once in a while, you could see a man or woman dressed in all black. More than likely a VC. Our problem was getting past the bridge without being seen.

We decided to just hole up here for the traffic to slow to a trickle. Anyone still on the bridge after midnight was undoubtedly a Viet Cong. While we were waiting, I checked on Cracker. I felt several places for a pulse but it was apparent that he was dead.

"Cracker's gone," I whispered to Baker.

"That sucks."

"If we could have gotten him to eat and drink he might have made it."

"Man, you did everything you could. Are we gonna' cut him loose?"

"No way. He comes with us."

"What's the point? He is dead. He doesn't care what happens from this point on," Baker replied.

"Because he is an American sailor and he deserves to be returned to where he came from."

"I think it's a waste of time," he said.

"And if it was you instead of Cracker?" I asked.

"Wouldn't make no difference to me. Dead is dead," he insisted.

I decided debating about it was a waste of time. Cracker was coming with us back to Ben Keo.

We were just about ready to make a break for it, slipping along the edge of the bank until we could get to the other side when a long line of gooks came hurrying along. There was an NVA officer leading them and he looked to be in a hurry. He was yelling at them to speed up. "Tăng tốc độ, tăng tốc độ," he kept saying. I didn't think to count them but I estimated there were at least two hundred VC that crossed the river. Someone was in for a rude awakening.

Once they were all passed, we waited a few more minutes. No one else crossed the bridge so we decided now was as good a time as any. We had to carry Cracker across the open expanse. It was only twenty or so yards but it seemed like a mile. We finally made it to a place where we could get back in the water. The foliage was even thicker here and that had its pros and cons.

It made hiding easier because of the way the trees and shrubs dipped right down to the water. The downside was that it made moving from one place to another much more difficult and time consuming. There were several places where we were forced to leave the cover of the undergrowth to get around the trees and vines. Every time we did this, it increased or chances of someone spotting us. I didn't like it but unfortunately there was no way around it. Our progress was really suffering. By sun-up we were only a few hundred yards upstream from the bridge. It was a good hiding area but it also meant we couldn't get out of the water to dry out.

We tied ourselves off so we wouldn't drift back down the river. It was as good a time as any to grab some shuteye. Within minutes I was sound asleep bobbing up and down in the water.

***

At Ben Keo everyone was working to get the base operational again. The boats had been hauled out of the water and were being repaired. The docking area was undergoing a total re-construction. Unfortunately, some of the heavy equipment that would have made the job easier, had been destroyed, slowing down the repair process.

The Captain had already chalked up the two missing PBR's and their crews as MIA's. His priority was to get the base operational as quickly as possible and that meant he wasn't about to waste resources searching for men that were most likely already dead.

Lieutenant Keeler was of a different mind. He wanted to get two boats up and running as quickly as possible. He felt that the Captain was more concerned about the dead VC rather than his own men.

"Chief, when can we get two of the PBR's up and running?"

"Another day or two. The men are working on it around the clock. It is the engine damage and replacing the 50's that is taking so long. We are in the process of dropping two rebuilt engines in and hooking everything up. The 50's and tub are being pulled out of one of the destroyed boats," he replied.

"Do you think they could still be alive?" Keeler asked.

"I honestly don't know at this point. It's going on four days and if they were hurt I would imagine they wouldn't be able to get back to base. They may float down river and hope they could get rescued by another base."

"Still. Ben is a big guy. If anyone could get the men home, it would be him," the Lieutenant replied.

"If he made it," the Chief added.

CHAPTER THIRTY-TWO

Things were starting to look more familiar now that we had passed under the bridge. I knew there was a large village less than a mile upstream from where we were now. That would be a difficult area for us to get by undetected. We knew that the VC often came to the village to get food.

It was still light by the time we got to the village. I knew there was no way for us to cross without being seen. We were going to have to wait until it got dark before we even made an attempt. Baker felt like we could make it right now but I told him there was no way we were going to try until the sun went down. We could smell them cooking which only made things harder for us. I had no idea how many were in the village, but it seemed from the noise that there were a hundred or more.

I looked at my watch, it was 0100 hours but the VC were still hanging around. I had hoped that they would be headed out on a mission. I knew that Baker was getting antsy but until the activity died down we simply couldn't risk it.

While we were waiting, it gave me a chance to think about what had happened with the two young VC. I had nonchalantly killed two young men without even thinking about it. It just seemed natural and that scared me. Is this what you turn into when you fight this kind of war? I hadn't even felt any remorse and I still didn't really. I mean, I was thinking about it, but I'd do it again in a heartbeat. It's one thing to be firing at the shoreline from a boat at the enemy but it's another to look him in the eye and take his life.

Yeah, I know the argument if I hadn't killed them they would've killed all of us. I've been in country less than seven months and I could already feel my attitude starting to change. What would I be like in another five months? Would killing become second nature? Would I turn into one of those guys that thought the only good gook was a dead gook?

The hours seemed to drag on forever and I kept hoping that the group of VCs' would eventually leave but they appeared to be staying in place. It was most unusual; they almost always went out at night looking for the enemy.

I whispered to Baker, "It looks like we are going to have to make a break for it."

"Man, that's crazy. They'll hear us for sure."

"Baker, we don't have another option."

"I know. It just sounds crazy. I don't see how we're going to do it without somebody noticing."

"All we can do is keep down, go slow, and try not to make much noise," I whispered, "I'll take Cracker across first and then let you know if it is still clear."

I ducked down as low as I could to the water, and started my way across the opening, pulling the dead body of Cracker along behind me. Once I got to the other side where there was some underbrush I tied him off. I stepped back into the opening to motion Baker that it was all clear.

He waved back, ducked down, and slowly started making his way across. He had gone no more than five or six feet when I heard someone coming down the path towards the river. Obviously, it had to be one of the VC. I frantically motioned for Baker to stop and duck down so that only his head was above the water.

I watched as a single VC came down to the river, turned around, and dropped his pants. Obviously, he was going to take care of business. I was no more than four feet from where he squatted. Not the best place in the world to be. I had no choice but to wait it out.

When he was finished, he pulled up his pants but instead of returning toward the camp, he turned and looked out toward the river. I knew it was just a matter of time before he spotted either me or Baker. I quickly reached up grabbed the VC by his shirt and pulled him in the water before he could even let out a sound. I immediately shoved his head under the water and tried holding him down. He was small, but he was wiry, and had more strength than I anticipated. I decided that all his thrashing around was causing too much noise, I felt I only had one option. I took my knife out of my scabbard and stabbed down until I found his body. He still fought and I did it again and again, until he finally lay still. I continued to hold him under water for a good minute before I finally let go of him. I pulled him up and shoved him out toward the current. I wanted his body to float downstream before he was missed by the other VC.

"Holy smokes," Baker said, coming up beside me, "Man, I didn't know whether to shit or get off the pot. I can't believe you pulled him in the water that fast. I was sure the other gooks would hear you and come running."

"We were extremely lucky. I don't think I could I held him down long enough to drown him. He was stronger than I thought. We need to get as far away from here as we can. It will be daylight in less than an hour and once they realize they have a man missing, they're going to come looking for what happened to him."

"Hopefully, his body will be far enough away that they won't come looking in our direction," Baker said.

"I don't think we should count on that."

"How much farther is it to the base?"

"Well, things are beginning to look familiar. If I had to guess I'd say we have eight or nine more miles to go. Ten at the outside," I told him.

"No way man, 10 miles? We can't make 10 more miles in this water. And doesn't the river get wider the closer we get to the base?"

"You're right about that, it does get wider, but that's a bridge we will have to cross when we get a lot farther up the river."

"The bridge we'll have to cross? I get it, that's a joke, right?"

"Does it look like I'm laughing?" I replied.

"Man, that sucks."

We began pushing farther upriver as the day grew brighter and brighter. Finally, the sun crested the horizon. A heavy mist lay on the river which was good for us. It meant that we were a little less visible. We continue to work our way closer to the base for about another hour before I felt that our chances of getting spotted were becoming too great.

My stomach was eating my backbone. I don't know which was worse the thirst or the hunger. We had been taking only small sips of water, trying to make it last. I knew one thing for sure we needed to get out of the water and rest. Hopefully, we could find something to eat or a source of water.

"Look, I'm gonna' leave you here with Cracker. I'm going to sneak up on the bank and see if I can find someplace where we could go and hide. We need to dry out and see if we can scavenge some food."

"I think we should go together," Baker said.

"No, you stay here. One of us needs to get back and let everyone know what happened. I stand a better chance on my own."

"And you will come back, right?" Baker asked.

"I'll just have a quick look around, if I run into any problems you'll know."

"Just hurry," Baker said.

I placed the magazine in the Ak and racked a round in the chamber. I slowly crawled up on the bank and after I'd gone no more than 10 yards, I raised up and could see a well-worn path. I looked in both directions but didn't see a thing. I decided it was worth the risk trying to get to the other side. I crouched low and ran as fast as I could and dove into the grass on the far side of the path.

I lay there panting. I was just sure that any VC in the area would be able to locate me by the thumping in my chest. All I could hear was my heartbeat. I lay there for several minutes looking up at the sky. The sun felt warm on my face, I must admit I felt like just lying there.

Finally, I decided I needed to get a move on. I worked my way deeper into the grass until it started to run into triple canopy. It was hard going but I continued to work my way toward the base. No more than 100 yards later I came to an opening where I could see Vietnamese women planting rice in their black pants, white tops, and conical hats. I saw no young males any place in the vicinity. It meant that if we want to travel overland for part of the way we would have to do it late at night. Also, we had the problem of Cracker still to consider. It wouldn't be easy dragging his body along.

To me this seemed like a real dilemma. We couldn't continue to stay in that water and not find food. We were both getting too weak, the lack of both food and water were becoming life-threatening. I worked my way back to where I had crossed the path. I decided at least we could get dry. I hustled across the path to where Baker waited.

"Come on," I said, "I found a place for us to dry out."

I realize something was totally wrong. Cracker's body was no longer tied to the branch. I looked at Baker but he was avoiding my gaze.

"Cracker, where is he?"

"He was just slowing us down. We were never going to make it back dragging him along. You wouldn't do it, so I decided to let him go."

For a minute I totally lost it. I pulled out my Colt 45 and pointed it at Baker's face.

"You son of a bitch. I should a waste you right here. Then I could let your body float down the river to join Cracker."

"Easy man, you know I'm right. We were never going to make it by pulling him along with us. It was too cumbersome and slow. If you really think about it. It was the best thing for all of us."

"That wasn't your call to make Baker," I said, my gun wavering as I pointed at his face.

I honestly felt at that moment like I could shoot the bastard. Finally, I calmed down and decided what was done was done. There was nothing I could do about it at this point.

"I'm going to go dry out," I said, and turned and sprinted back across the path to lie in the sun.

I didn't wait nor care if Baker join me. I lay there letting the sun warm my body. I close my eyes I let my mind go totally blank. A minute or so later Baker flopped down beside me. I didn't bother to acknowledge him. There was nothing I could say that was going to make the situation better. He started to say something two or three times, but I guess he thought better of it, finally he laid back to soak in the sun.

At some point, I must've drifted off. My eyes snapped open when I heard voices coming up the trail. I listened intently and realized they were VC. I could hear them laughing and talking amongst themselves. I slowly reached over and placed my hand over Baker's mouth, he startled awake but I held my finger to my lips. I pointed to where the sound was coming from. He nodded his head in acknowledgment. I pointed to the triple canopy and indicated that we needed to get back in there and hide. He nodded he understood.

We crawled on our bellies slowly until we reached the tree line. It was apparent that the VC had stopped by the river. We could hear them talking and laughing like they didn't have a care in the world. I sure couldn't say the same for us.

CHAPTER THIRTY-THREE

The VC lingered by the water until almost sunset. The hard part for us, besides waiting, was the smell of a food that they were cooking. It was all we could do to not rush out there and try to take them on.

When they finally left and we could no longer hear their voices, I said to Baker, "Well that's changes our plans."

"What do you mean by that?", Baker asked.

"I was hoping we could travel overland for a while, but obviously, with the VC ahead of us that doesn't seem like a very good idea."

"So we're going to have to get back in the water?"

"I'm afraid so; I just don't see another option."

"Geez, I hate that, but I understand where you're coming from."

"We're still going to have to be very careful. We have no idea if they set up an ambush along the trail."

We hurried across the path and slid into the water. For some reason, the water seemed colder than before. I'm sure it was just my imagination.

While it still didn't make it right, Baker was correct about one thing, our progress was much faster without having to drag Cracker along with us. As we were rounding a bend the singsong voices of the Vietnamese came drifting our way. It was impossible to tell how many there were, but from the level of noise, I felt it had to be a big contingent.

"That doesn't sound very good," Baker said.

"Not at all," I answered.

"Should we just wait here?" He asked.

"Let's go a little farther, maybe you can see how many there are," I said.

"Why? What's the point? We can't do anything about it."

"We could see if this is a temporary camp or one that they use permanently. If it's permanent, we can report it when we get back to Ben Keo," I replied.

"*If*, we get back."

I was beginning to like Baker less and less. He was one of the most negative people I've ever met. He could complain better than anyone I had ever met. The problem with that is, after a while it starts to drag on you. I was at that point.

"I'll tell you what Baker, if you don't want to go along with me you're free to head out on your own. One thing I can tell you for sure is that I'm sick your belly aching. So, if you're sticking with me, shut your damn mouth or else take off," I told him.

He started to say something and evidently thought better of it and just kept his mouth shut. I didn't even bother to look back, I just slowly started toward where the VC were. We went about 200 yards further and I could smell food cooking. I was surprised that they had no noise discipline. Usually Charlie didn't say very much, especially during the day when our S & D patrols were out. I wondered if they were just one part of a much larger group. It's the only thing that made sense to me. I was beginning to wonder if they were amassing to try to overrun Ben Keo

"Do you know what they're saying?" Baker asked.

"I can pick some of it up but my Vietnamese leaves a lot to be desired," I told him.

"Man, yours is a lot better than mine, which is practically non-existent. I just know Boom-Boom, and a few other bar phrases," Baker said.

"I doubt that will do us much good in these circumstances."

We crept a little closer. I was trying to make out some of the words. The only thing I heard clearly was "Thời gian để đi. Nhanh lên", which roughly means it's time to go, or at least that's what I thought.

"What are they saying?" Baker asked.

"I think they're getting ready to take off," I replied.

"Hey, that's good. That means we should be able to get moving pretty soon," Baker said.

"Maybe we're going to get a little luck for a change," I said.

I looked at my watch and saw that it was going on 1830. I decided we needed to give them at least 45 minutes to get out of the area before we moved again. We waited and could hear the sounds of ol' Charlie getting further and further away.

"You ready?" I asked Baker.

"Man, the sooner the better," was his reply.

We made our way slowly upriver. I stopped every few hundred yards and listened for any sounds. For the first time, I was sure where we were. I figured we had less than two miles to go before we reached the area directly across from the base. We still had one obstacle to overcome. We were on the wrong side of the river which meant that we were going to have to find a way to traverse it. I'm a strong swimmer and wasn't too worried about making it to the other side.

"Baker, how good are you at swimming?"

"I don't know, okay I guess."

"Are you a strong enough swimmer to get to the other side of the river?" I asked him.

"Whoa, I said I was okay, but I'm sure not an Olympic swimmer. I mean, that's pretty far to go," he said.

"Well, our vests are pretty waterlogged. I don't think they're going to do us much good. I don't see any other way for us to get across but to swim."

"How far do you think it is across the river?" He asked.

"I'm guessing around a half mile, maybe a little more."

"Geez, I don't think I can swim that far," Baker replied.

"All right, no use worrying about it now, we will worry about that when the time comes."

We continued upriver stopping occasionally, to listen for any voices. It was going on 0100 hrs. when I could see the lights at Ben Keo. It had been a long hard trip but were finally nearing our destination.

"That's Ben Keo across the river," I told Baker.

"That looks a lot farther than a half a mile to me," Baker said.

"It is what it is, we'll just have to make the best of it," I replied.

"That's easy for you to say, you must be a pretty good swimmer. I on the other hand, don't think I can make it that far," Baker said.

"Look, we've come this far. I only see two options at this point. The first is that we try to get across together. I'll try to help you if you get in trouble. The second option, is for me to swim over while you stay here."

"Oh yeah, like that's going to happen."

"Hey, if you've got another option, now's the time to tell me," I told Baker.

I could see that he was struggling with what to do. He didn't like the idea of being left alone, but he was smart enough to realize that it would be a real struggle for him to swim that far.

He stood there weighing his options for several moments.

Finally, he said, "I don't think I can swim that far. I guess I have no choice but to wait here. I don't like it, but I just don't see that I have any other option."

"I honestly think that's the right decision," I told him.

I slipped off my vest, my shoes, and pants, and handed Baker the AK-47 along with my Colt.45.

"I'll have someone come and get you just as soon as I can. I figure it's going to take me at least half an hour to get across the river. I don't know how long it will take to get a boat headed to pick you up, but it shouldn't take more than an hour."

"Just make it as fast as you can," Baker said.

"I'll do the best I can. If no one's here to pick you up in a couple of hours, that means I didn't make it across the river, and you're going to have to find your own way across."

"Man, don't even talk like that."

"Hey, you have to face the reality that that could possibly happen," I said.

"I got a better idea, just make it, and get somebody over here as fast as you can," Baker replied.

"I'll do as fast as I can," I promised him.

We shook hands and I slid into the water and began swimming across the broad river.

CHAPTER THIRTY-FOUR

The first part of the swim wasn't too bad. The water was calm and I was making pretty good time. Toward the middle of the river the current kicked in and it got more difficult from that point on. I didn't realize how far downstream I was being carried. I kept trying to correct by keeping my eye on Ben Keo.

Between not having enough to eat and hypothermia from being in the water so long, I found that I was tiring more quickly than I had expected. No matter how hard I fought it, I was slowly being swept downstream.

I kept trying to compensate but no matter how hard I tried I was losing ground. I have always prided myself on being a strong swimmer but now I found I was losing the battle. I rolled over on my back trying to rest for a few minutes but the current was carrying me downstream even faster. As tired as my arms where, I knew I had no choice but to try to make it to the shore. I started swimming again.

It was kind of like those incidences where no matter how hard to you try you still seem to be the same distance off. I finally made it to where the water started to smooth out again. From there it became easier and after what seemed like a lifetime I made it to where I could stand up. I slogged ashore and fell on the bank gasping for air.

I rested for a few minutes before I stood up and started walking toward the base. I had been swept down river about half mile. I looked at my watch and realized that it had taken me almost an hour to get across the river.

When I finally got to the base, the guards, standing with their rifles pointed at me, weren't sure who I was. I was standing there naked, looking like a drowned rat. They were pointing their M-16s at me and demanding the password for the day.

I almost broke out laughing. Password for the day? Hell, I didn't even know what day it was. It took some explaining but I finally convinced them that I really was an American and belonged to the base. To verify that, they sent for Lt. Keeler. I could tell that he was shocked at seeing me still alive.

"Man, oh man, are you a sight for sore eyes. Geez you look like hell. How can you even see out of your eyes, they are so swollen?"

"You can't begin to imagine how good it is to almost see you again," I replied.

"The same goes on this end," Keeler replied.

The guards opened the gate and I stepped inside. It was a funny feeling since I wasn't sure I'd ever see Ben Keo again.

"LT. Keeler, Baker made it as well, but he didn't think he could swim across the river. I told him as soon as I got over here I'd send someone to pick him up."

"I'll get a team together immediately. Unfortunately, that means I'll have to send you back out to guide them. I hate to do it to you but there's no other way they could find him."

"I understand. The sooner we retrieve him the better we all will feel," I replied.

Within ten minutes, dressed in clean clothes, I found myself climbing back on a PBR. Honestly, it was the last thing I wanted to do at the moment. We headed out back across the river and I directed him to where I had left Baker. Everyone was pretty tense because they knew that Charlie had been hanging out in that area. We drifted in to where I had left Baker.

"Baker," I whispered as loud as I dared.

No reply came back. I tried it several more times and still nothing. I was certain we were at the right place where I had entered the water. I got out of the boat and waded to the shoreline. I scouted out the area where I left them. I was just about to leave when I saw the two AK-47s and my Colt .45 lying on the ground along with my clothes. His life vest and shoes were sitting on the shore. The only thing I could think of was that he decided to take off and try to swim the river.

I grabbed up the gear and got back on the boat.

"He's not there. I found his gear and I can only assume that he decided to try and swim the river. I don't think he realizes how strong the current is in the middle of the river. If he tried it I'm pretty sure he would've been swept pretty far down the river, assuming he didn't drown."

"I'm going to send out a couple boats to see if we can find him. At the very least we should recover his body. I'm not going to ask you to go along, I want you to get checked out. I'm going to send for medevac and have you taken back for complete physical before you return to duty," LT. Keeler said.

"I'm fine, I think I should be on one of the boats. After all, he was one of my crewman."

"That may be true, but you're not going out again until you're checked out," the Lieutenant insisted.

I thought about arguing some more but I was pretty sure it was a lost cause. The LT was just looking after me. He is a good guy, and he just wanted to make sure I was okay before returning to duty.

He walked me back to the hooch which was now totally empty. It was strange. All my crew members were now dead or missing. I sat down on the edge of my cot, folded my arms across my knees, and lay my head down. I was having a hard time coming to grips with why I was still alive and everyone else was dead. What made me so special? I hadn't done anything different than the other guys and yet here I was. Now I knew how Dog felt when he survived and the others didn't.

I didn't have much time to ponder it. I could hear a chopper coming up the river. I grabbed a few things to take with me and waited for it to land on the low pad. The LT came over, patted me on the back, and told me that was the medevac and that he didn't want to see me again until the medical team released me. I didn't say anything I just walked over and climbed on the slick. Thirty seconds later I was on my way to the medical ship.

We were following the Delta and I couldn't help but look out and see if I could spot anything below. I knew it was futile but I had to at least try to spot any of our men. The flight took longer than twenty-minutes before we landed on the LST Harriet County. I was right back where I had been just a month or so before. I walked down to sick bay and reported in as ordered.

"Well, well, the prodigal son returns," Ensign Peterson said, smiling as I walked up.

"You know, this is the second time I've been ordered to be checked out."

"I hope you're not complaining, I checked you out pretty thoroughly last time," she said.

"I have to admit, that part was pretty fantastic."

"Then I just may have to give you another exam," she said, rubbing against me, as she walked back to sick bay with me in tow.

When I saw what I looked like in the mirror, I wondered why she would even be interested in me. My face was swollen from all of the bug bites. Several places had ugly sores where the leeches had attached to my back and arms. They didn't even bother to take my clothes off, they just grabbed a pair of scissors and cut them off.

I don't know how many vials of blood they drew but I was surprised that they could even find any after all the mosquito bites. They checked me out from the top of my head to my toes. They took x-rays of my chest just to make sure that everything was okay. I had a complete physical and was pronounced in fairly good shape, all things considered.

"I'm ordering you to stay on board for at least four days and get bed rest. At the end of four days I'll reevaluate you to see if you can be released back to duty," the doctor said.

"Sir, I lost all of my crew. I need to get back to the base to help search for them," I told him.

"Son, I appreciate that, but there's no way I'm going to release you after what you've been through until I'm sure you're physically okay. Arguing isn't going to change a thing. They're going to have to do the search without you," he said and walked off.

A nurse brought me a set of scrubs to wear and exchanged them for the sheet that they had draped over me. I was taken back to the same bunk room that I had been in previously. There were seven other guys in there. Most of them had been pretty badly wounded. I felt fairly silly standing there with just a few bandages on. They probably thought I was a real pansy.

I decided the heck with it, found a bunk, and laid down. I was asleep almost before my head hit the pillow. I don't know what time it was when I was awakened by a nurse with a tray of food.

"What time is it?", I asked rubbing my eyes.

"0600 hrs." was her reply.

"How long have I been out?".

"Almost 12 hours."

Wow, I knew I had been out for a while, but I never imagined it had been 12 hours. She handed me the tray of food and I began wolfing it now.

"Take it easy," she said, "if you eat too much too fast you will just throw it back up. You need to go slowly. When your stomach feels full, stop for a while. I know you're starved but eating too fast will just make you sick."

I did as she said, even though it was hard. I couldn't believe how hungry I was. I had to force myself to slow down. I looked at my left arm for the first time realized I had an IV in it.

"What's that for?", I asked.

"Saline solution. Even though you were in the water for five days you were still dehydrated. Being in the water and having water to drink or two totally different things."

While she was explaining that I suddenly started feeling nauseous. Obviously, she had been right. It was all I could do to keep from regurgitating.

She handed me a barf pan, and said, "You don't look very well, I think you're gonna' need this."

I fought it for as long as I could, but it was a losing battle, and I lost almost everything I had just consumed. Here I was barfing my guts out in front of a nurse, I felt like a total jerk.

"Geez, I'm sorry. I was just so hungry."

"No big deal, it happens all the time," she said.

I lay back in the bed feeling like total moron. She said it was no big deal, but it was to me. She sat the food tray on a stand beside me and took the barf pan off to empty. When she came back I felt slightly better.

"I'm going to leave the food with you. You'll probably drift off when you wake back up you'll be hungry again. Just remember, small bites and chew them well. Don't rush it, there's plenty more food for that came from," she told me.

I closed my eyes, and before I even realized it, I was sound asleep. Unfortunately, the sleep was short-lived. I sat up, soaking wet from sweating. I had been reliving those fatal moments when Big Ben's boat had been hit with the RPG's. I could still see the bodies being thrown out of the boat and tossed in the air like rag dolls.

CHAPTER THIRTY-FIVE

I finally managed to rejoin the living early the next morning. My watch indicated 06:10. I was just pulling back the sheet when Ensign Peterson came walking in.

"Hey sailor, long time no see. You never write or call," she said smiling.

"Hardy-har. I'm too busy getting my butt shot off," I shot back.

"And a fine one it is, if I do say so myself."

"Awe shucks, ma'am. You probably say that to all the sailors," I joked back.

"So, they tell me you were in the water five days trying to get back to base while avoiding the VC," she said, seriously.

"I've had better times, that's for sure. I was lucky, unfortunately, none of my other crew members were," I replied.

"Still, the fact that you survived is pretty darn amazing."

"I sure don't feel amazing. I didn't keep my men alive and looking out for them is one of my prime duties."

"Martin, you can't beat yourself up over something like that. This is war. People get killed. Ben, the guy with the most experience, didn't make it either. You must let this go or you will get yourself killed. You don't get to choose who lives or dies. You may have some responsibility but the ultimate choice is up to a higher authority. You may not like it but that is the way it is," she told me.

I knew she was right but I still felt the guiltiest about Baker. I didn't particularly like him as a person, but he was one of my men. He was alive when I decided to swim across the Mekong. Maybe if I had just waited until the sun was up and he could see my progress he might have waited. Of course, I knew the fallacy in that plan. Every gook on the river would have spotted me and I would never have made it before someone used me for target practice.

"Come on. You need to get out of bed and do some walking," Peterson told me.

I stood up in just my shorts and dressed while she continued to eye me, never looking away. Damn woman. Once I finished dressing she told me to follow her. We ended up on the main deck and walked to the fantail. Leaning over the rail and looking out at Vietnam it was striking how beautiful and peaceful it looked from the South China Sea.

"It looks like paradise doesn't?" She said.

"Sure, if you're on a boat this far out it's great. It's a totally different picture once you get into the Delta. There danger lurks around every bend. One moment it can be routine, and the next you find yourself in a fight for your life."

"I don't know how you guys do that. I mean, the tension must be enormous," Peterson said.

"So why are you here in Vietnam?" I asked her.

"I was a military brat. It's really been the only life I've ever known. When I was in the sixth or seventh grade I remember asking my dad what school would I be going to next year? He just said wherever he was sent."

"He must be very proud of you," I told her.

"I suppose he is in his own way. I mean, my dad was in the Army, and he was a little upset to find I joined the Navy."

"Yikes, that's a little harsh."

"Not really, he never had a son, and I think he was proud of the fact that I became a commissioned officer."

"He didn't tell you that?"

"He did in his own way. My dad wasn't big on a lot of words," she replied.

"Why do you think we are here in Vietnam in the first place?" I asked her.

"A lot of reasons. These people need our help. We are the only ones that can stabilize this country," she said.

"Barbra. They don't want us here. There is nothing that the US can offer them. They don't want our kind of democracy. All we are doing is making their lives harder. This is a Civil War and we need to leave it to them to resolve it," I insisted.

"I honestly can't agree but I'm not out among them. I don't see what you see. Maybe if I did, it would be different.

I don't know how long we stood there just watching the sun glistening off the water, but it was the first time since I had been in Vietnam that I felt totally at peace. At some point, she reached over and took my hand.

"Hey, no pressure, but if you would like to meet at the same place we did last time... I know, I would really enjoy spending more time with you."

"Just name the time."

"2200 hrs.?" she replied.

"It works for me. You can count on me being there," I assured her.

"Good, I'll see you then. I need to get back before they start looking for me."

I watched as she walked away. Given the choice between looking at Vietnam and the shape of Ensign Peterson walking off, it was no contest.

After she disappeared I sat there daydreaming about what the evening would bring. I was brought back to reality by my name being hailed over the loudspeaker. I was being told to report to the captain's quarters. Now what, I wondered? Whatever it was, I was hoping it wouldn't interfere with this evening's plans.

I headed up to officer's quarters and knocked on the door to the captain's state room.

"Come," was the reply from the other side of the door.

I opened the door, and said, "Machinist Mate first class, Martin French, reporting as ordered sir,"

"Come in first class French. At ease, take a seat."

I'd seen the captain around the ship on several occasions, but this was the first time I had ever actually been face-to-face with him. He sat behind his desk in a starched white shirt that had the first button undone. He had salt-and-pepper hair, and deep crow's feet around his eyes, probably from squinting out at the ocean.

"First class French, it's a pleasure to meet you. I've heard all about your sojourn back to the base. It's hard to believe anyone could have lasted five days in the water while avoiding the VC. I was also informed about your attempt to save two of your crew members. It's my understanding that one of the men succumbed to his injuries, and the other man probably drowned while trying to cross the Delta," the captain said.

"Yes sir."

"How did you avoid capture?" the captain asked.

"By staying in the water and following the riverbank," I replied.

"Still, dragging the other two along must have taken a terrible toll on your strength."

"I had no choice. They were from my crew and most importantly, they were American sailors. I only did what

I hope they would have done for me," I told the captain.

I wasn't sure about the last part. I doubt Baker would have given it much thought about cutting both Cracker and I lose rather than trying to drag us along. Still, I didn't want to say that to the captain.

"Your dedication is admirable. I have decided to nominate you for a second Bonze Star. The first one was changed to a Meritorious Service medal. I intend to see you get the Bronze Star this time. I've already forwarded the appropriate paperwork. Well done machinist mate first class Martin French."

"Sir, I didn't do anything more than any other sailor would've done."

"Son, what the Navy needs is more sailors like you. Some of the replacements we are getting now days leave a lot to be desired," the Captain said, "Well done sailor."

"Aye aye sir, thank you."

"I'll inform you when the medal becomes official. You're dismissed first class French. Get rested up before you go back in the field."

I'll have to admit I was in a state of shock when I left the captain's office. The last thing I expected was getting a medal for just trying to survive. My getting back to base was self-preservation more than anything else.

I realized that I had not eaten all day. I decided to go to the galley and grab a bite then go back to my bunk and rest. If tonight was anything like the last time I made love to Barbara, I was going to need plenty of strength.

They say that the Navy has the best food of any military service. What I had for lunch, was proof of that. I had pork chops, mashed potatoes, gravy, corn, and peach cobbler for dessert. I doubt any other military branch was having a meal like that.

Once I finished my meal, I headed back to the sleeping birth, stripped down to my shorts, and crawled in my rack. Unfortunately, I didn't fall asleep immediately. My mind kept drifting to later that evening.

I was surprised that Barbara was already there waiting for me. I figured she would be late like last time. The other big surprise was that she had on her dress whites.

"Wow, you look fantastic," I said looking her over.

"Thank you kind sir, I just thought that you might want to see what I look like dressed as a woman."

"All I can say is that you look beautiful standing there."

I looked around and found that she had laid out a large blanket. She had laid it out so that we would not be visible unless somebody came looking for us.

We sat and talked about a variety of topics. Everything from Vietnam to what our lives were like when we were growing up were discussed. When we finally made love, it was different from last time. While still intense, we were slower and took time to discover each other's body. We made love five or six times in the two hours that we had together.

"Martin, this has been fantastic, but I can't risk my career getting caught. I'm an officer and you're an enlisted man. That means I could get court martialed for what we are doing," she said.

"I know, I was actually surprised you went through with it this time," I replied.

"Martin, I really, really like you, and if the circumstances were different I would like to spend as much time as possible with you. It's just that..."

"I understand, there is no need to say anything else. Being court martialed is not an option for anyone. My orders have been cut and I'm leaving in two days. We both enjoyed the time we had together. Let's just leave it at that."

"Maybe when..."

"Don't. There are no guarantees about what can happen tomorrow. There's no use speculating on the future. The best thing for both of us is just to remember our time together."

CHAPTER THIRTY-SIX

As I was climbing on the helicopter to head back to base, I looked over at the superstructure and saw Barbara standing there. She waved, threw me a kiss, and disappeared through one of the hatches.

Flying over Ben Keo I immediately saw that there had been a lot of effort going into fortifications. All the trees within 100 yards had been cleared. The perimeter fence had been beefed up with hundreds of yards of barbed wire. Two new towers had been constructed. Mortars had been placed on jeeps along with 50 caliber machine guns. They had also acquired a third Huey.

The docks had been totally rebuilt, with lookout towers facing the river in case of attack from the far side of the Delta. If the VC were going to overrun Ben Keo it certainly wasn't going to be a walk in the park. It would be nothing like the last time.

When I got out of the helicopter I headed to the CP to check in. A new personnel man that I had never seen before was sitting behind a rickety desk.

"Martin French, first class machinist mate, reporting back for duty," I said, and handed him my orders.

"Whoa, you are *the* Martin French that survived for five days in NVA country?"

"That very Martin French."

"Lieutenant Keeler wanted to be notified the moment you came back. Hang on while I ring him up."

I had forgotten how bloody hot it was after spending time on the ship. By the time the LT showed up, my shirt was sticking to my body.

"Well, well, the prodigal child returns. Good to have you back Martin," LT. Keeler said, shaking my hand.

"Thank you, sir, I am more than ready to get back to action."

"Well as you can see we've been pretty busy around here. There's been a lot of talk of another large VC offensive. We've been getting conflicting reports, but it's better to be safe than sorry," Keeler replied.

"I'm all for that. What can I do to help?"

"Do you feel like you're up for captaining another PBR?"

"The sooner I get back, the better it will be. All I need is a crew," I told him.

"Believe it or not, that's not a problem," he said.

I followed him down to the pier and we jumped on to one of the PBR's tied up. There were four guys that stood up when the LT. and I came on board.

"Guys, this is your new captain, machinist mate first class Martin French. He's been with us before he just returned from short stay in hospital. French, this is your new crew. Second class engineman, Frank Bauer. That skinny little guy is Iggy Mason. Iggy is the third-class signalman. The big guy is John E. Johnson, radioman second class. And last but not least, Sammy Foster, boatswain's mate third class. Alright, I'll let you guys get acquainted. You don't need me around," Keeler said, and turned and left.

There was kind of an awkward silence for a few seconds and then I decided we needed to get to know each other.

"Okay I can figure out some of it, I get Iggy, but do you just go by that name?"

"Yeah, there's not a lot of nicknames for somebody who already has a name like Iggy," he replied.

"They usually just call me J.J." Johnson said.

"That makes a lot of sense. Any nickname yet Frank?"

"Not really, people usually just call me Bauer, no first name," he said.

"That's pretty easy to remember. What about you Sammy?" I asked.

"Sammy works fine for me," he said.

"On my last boat, the crew gave me the nickname of Iceman," I told them.

"Yeah, we've heard quite a few stories about you already. We were told you were given that name because you are always cool under fire. You never let anything rattle you. All I can say is I'm glad you're our Captain," Iggy replied.

"Guys, all I can tell you is that the most important thing on this boat is you. I put my crew before everything else. In war there are always casualties, but I can promise you that I'll do everything in my power to get you guys home safely."

They were all shaking their heads in agreement and stealing glances at each other. I wasn't just blowing smoke, I had already lost enough lives, and while I knew it was always the possibility that I'd lose more, I needed to assure them that I wouldn't gamble with their lives.

"You guys don't know a thing about me..."

"More than you realize. We have heard a lot of stories of some of the things you have pulled off besides staying alive for five days in the water while deep in VC country," JJ said.

"Don't believe everything you hear. I'm sure some of it was true but some of it was probably exaggerated."

We sat on the stern and just talked for the next two hours. I asked a few questions and found they were up to speed on how to handle about anything that was thrown at us. The only tense moment was when Sammy and Bauer got into a philosophical discussion about why we are here in Vietnam. Iggy was of the opinion that if we pulled out, the whole country would turn Communist. Bauer didn't give a shit as long as he got out of here alive. He felt it was their war and we had no place in it. I kept my mouth shut and just listened. The argument wasn't heated but both felt they were right.

Bauer's point was; you can't force people to accept help. They wanted nothing we offered. We represented nothing more than an additional hardship. Iggy was one of those *'we need to win the hearts and minds'* of *the people.* Good luck with that.

***

Our first mission as a crew was the midnight to noon patrol. I watched as they went through the pre-check and was pleased with how competently they went about the task.

The other boat captain was Brian Miller and had been in-country three months. He seemed sharp and judging from our conversations, knew what to do when the SHTF. I would be the lead boat and he would follow fifty yards or so behind.

The first part of the patrol was about as dull as it could get. Nothing was stirring as we motored along. We were in a different section of the river than I had previously patrolled so I was probably the most tense.

At 02:25 that changed when Iggy spotted a group of VC running along the riverbank. He immediately opened fire with the M60 and everyone started firing, following his tracers. Within seconds both boats were blasting away. There was little cover for them and we were able to put a hurt on them. They finally managed to slip into the night.

I had already called in a sit-rep, and of course the Captain wanted a body count. While not the best thing, I motored over to the other boat and we tied off.

"You heard the Captain. He wants a body count," I told Brian.

"He is frickin' crazy. That's all he cares about. Body count. He doesn't seem to care if it's our bodies on the line," he replied.

"Hey man, you're singing to the choir. What do you think we should do?" I asked him.

"Iceman, you're the lead. I'll do whatever you say."

"Did your people hear the Captain?" I asked.

"I doubt it. I just barely caught it myself," Brian responded.

"Okay. I think it's stupid to take the risk. We have no idea how many are out there and if they have set up an ambush. I'm going to wait a half hour and then call in a sit-rep. I'll tell them we counted twenty-five bodies and lots of blood trails."

"Better make it forty-one or he will want a second count."

I said, "Forty-one it is. I like the odd number. Sounds better."

Brian and I worked out a story so it would match if it came to that. Thirty-five minutes later I called into LT. Keeler and told him we had counted forty-one gooks dead and a lot of blood trails. He sounded somewhat amused but said that he would pass it on to the Captain.

As he was signing off he said, "Make sure your stories match."

The LT. was no fool. He knew damn well we weren't about to go ashore at night just to get our asses shot off so the Captain could be happy. I figured he would probably stall the appropriate amount of time before reporting to the Captain.

Once we were done, we untied and resumed our patrol. Nothing further happened during the night. When the sun came up we went about the usual searching of the sampans. It was just another boring day in Vietnam. All that was accomplished was that I was one day shorter than before.

You find that nothing really matters. Not the season, holidays, or anything else. The only clock you care about is how much time remains in-country. Every day you survive is a good day and one less until you rotate back to the real world.

Of course, the flip side was that at any moment your number could come up and you would be going home sooner than expected. Unfortunately, you would be in a coffin in the back of a C-130 Hercules.

Given a choice, I would rather count down the days. When we got in at noon, the Lieutenant was at the pier waiting for us. I wasn't sure what that meant but it did concern me.

"Patrol go okay except for the skirmish last night?" he asked.

"Yes sir," I replied.

"Make sure your after-action report notes that you counted the bodies twice to get an accurate number, understand?"

"Twice, yes sir, understood."

"Make sure Miller notes that as well."

"Will do LT. Thank you, sir," I replied.

"You're a smart boat captain Iceman. You know how to take care of your men," he replied and headed back up the pier.

And you are a smart Officer, I thought to myself as I watched him walk away.

CHAPTER THIRTY-SEVEN

We were all down on the boat just shooting the bull when the LT came down.

"Iceman, everyone is to be in a clean uniform. Admiral Wyler is coming in for an award ceremony at 1600 hours. No boats will be on patrol until the ceremony is over," he told us.

I asked, "What kind of ceremony?"

"Well, the kind where all the men will be in clean uniforms. All except you. You will be in your dress whites. Your medals have come through. You will be receiving three medals today."

"Three? I don't get it. What three?"

"The Bronze Star, Meritorious Service Medal, and the Purple Heart."

"Wait. That's crazy. Purple Heart? For what?" I asked.

"Looked at your ear recently?"

"Hell, sir. That was just a scratch. That isn't a real wound," I argued.

"Evidently someone thought it was. No used arguing. Just have your men there by 15:45. Admiral Wyler likes to hear himself talk so it may take a while."

"Whoa. You are one badass hero," Sammy said.

"Wow," Frank added.

"It's a bunch of BS," I replied.

"Sounds righteous to me my man," JJ added.

"Purple Heart for a little shot off of my ear? What a crock," I replied.

"Hey, my main man, you got one hell of an ugly ear. That shit is going to be with you the rest of your life." Iggy chimed in.

There was nothing left to be said. It is what it is. We all made our way back to the hooch to get ready. I dug out my dress whites. They weren't too bad all things considered.

While I was getting dressed, Lieutenant Keeler came to talk to me.

"Just so you know, this is a photo op for the Admiral and Captain. They will have a gaggle of camera people with them so they can get into the news. Supporting our boys on the front line, and all of that. Just nod and salute. Whatever you do, don't talk to the press about how the war is going."

"What do I say, if they ask?"

"Tell them you only see your small patch of the war and from where you sit, it's going well," the LT replied.

"And if they press further?"

"I'll step in and pull you out. I'll be right at your elbow as soon as the

Admiral gets done pinning the medals on you."

"I would really appreciate that. Thanks Lieutenant," I replied.

We all sat in the hooch waiting for the Admiral to arrive. It gave me a chance to learn a little more about my crew. For instance, JJ was arrested for statutory rape. His girlfriend was seventeen and her parents pressed charges. The judge gave him an ultimatum of three years in jail or join the military. He joined the Navy.

Sammy came from West Virginia and was destined to become a coal miner. He just couldn't see that as a way of life so he joined the Navy. Frank Bauer dropped out of College and joined before he was drafted. He did not want to be in the Army. Iggy joined to get away from an abusive father and a worthless mother. They were both alcoholics and druggies. In that hour I, learned a lot about the men I was spending my life with.

"Chopper," Iggy said, suddenly standing.

"Yep. Must be the Admiral. Let me take a look at you," JJ said, turning me around and inspecting me.

He straightened my sailor tie before pronouncing me ready to go.

We all headed out to the CP where the ceremony was to take place. I was glad to see the Lieutenant already there. He motioned for me to come stand by him.

The rest of the base personnel were to line up facing me and the Lieutenant. The Captain stepped out of the CP in full dress whites.

"We will all salute the Admiral at once, understood?"

Well duh.

We could see the chopper kicking up dust as it settled down on the helo pad. A second one landed a minute later. We waited as a contingent of people made their way toward us. The reporters were practically falling over each other. It was all I could do to keep from laughing.

The Lieutenant yelled, "Attention on Deck" and we all snapped to attention.

The Captain saluted and we all followed suit. It wasn't as sharp as the Captain wanted, I'm sure.

"Admiral Wyler, on behalf of the men, I would like to extend a welcome to Ben Keo," the Captain said.

"Captain Willard, it's a pleasure to meet these fine sailors fighting for the liberation of South Vietnam. It's a special pleasure to be here today to present three medals to one of our gallant sailors. Blah...blah...blah."

The cameras rolled and clicked as he rattled on for a good ten minutes. Finally, he got around to calling me forward. He pinned on the three medals, shook my hand, and told me what an honor it was to have men like me serving in the Navy and doing such a contribution to the future freedom of Vietnam. He saluted, I saluted and that was pretty much it in a nutshell. I wasn't asked to say a single word.

The Admiral, Captain, and Lieutenant held a pow-wow while we were heading back to our hooch to change back to work clothes. My guys were giving me a good-natured razzing about how much weight I was carrying. We changed into our dungarees and as I stepped outside, the LT was waiting for me.

"Congratulations French. Damned impressive," he said shaking my hand.

"I'm just glad that's over," I replied.

"Well not exactly. It seems the Admiral wants his adjunct to go on a combat mission so he can get a few medals. The Captain thinks you should be the one to take him along on a mission that has just come up," he said looking down.

"A mission that has just come up? And take along his adjunct so he can play real sailor?"

"Not my idea but...well there it is."

"There it is."

***

The LT went and brought Lieutenant Bollard to the boat and introduced us to him.

"Have you ever been on a PBR before?" I asked him.

"Definitely not. I've been on a few yachts and a couple of sail boats but nothing like this," he said pointing to our boat.

"What about firing your weapon or one of the 30's?"

"Just during qualifying".

"But not at a person?" I asked.

"No."

"Alright. You were at the briefing. We are taking supplies and ammo to Nan Ke Lo another base sixty klicks upriver. They are in sustained contact with the VC. We are to get the supplies to them and help in any way we can. There will be four boats going, which is unusual in and of itself. Once we get there, just do whatever anyone tells you to do," I said.

"Wait. You mean follow enlisted men's orders?"

"That's what I said."

"Maybe you don't understand. I'm a Lieutenant and you are a Petty Officer. I don't take orders from enlisted personnel," he said placing his hands on his hips.

"You listen to me Lieutenant. When we are on this boat, I am the Captain. I'm in charge. Not you or anyone else. You will do what I tell you to do for two reasons. I've already mentioned one. The other is that if you don't you are going to die. You can either accept that or get off the ship."

"You cannot talk to..."

"I already have. Make up your mind. If you are going, sit down and do what you are told," I said.

I called the other boat Captains and made sure we were ready to go and all guns were locked and loaded. Once everyone called in, we headed out full bore for the Base and Nan Ke Lo.

We were maintaining around thirty-five yards between each craft. The plan was to unload one boat at a time while the rest covered the base.

Once one was off loaded, the second one would go in and off load and continue until we were finished. We would then stay on station to support the base as long as they needed.

We could hear the fight before we rounded the last bend. Two Hueys were hammering away while circling the area. This had to be a sustained firefight to have lasted this long.

"Okay. I will go in first and unload. The rest of you do what you can to support the base," I said over the Mic.

"Are you going in there?" the Lieutenant said, pointing at the pier.

Bullets were splashing all around the pier and the buildings next to them. Just as I turned to head in, he jumped in the cabin looking deathly white.

"Do not go in there. This is crazy. We need to find another way to get them supplies. We can order an air drop," he yelled, panic stricken, "I am giving you a direct order. Do not go in there."

He started to raise his weapon at me but both JJ and Sammy aimed theirs at him.

"Bad Idea. You shoot me and they will blow your head off," I said.

"I'll have you court martialed," he screamed.

"Lieutenant, get out of my cabin. Get your weapon and get ready to use it against the VC," I said and started into the pier.

I was no longer paying attention to him, I was focused on determining the best way to get to the pier and unload.

We could see the tracers and muzzle flashes as we raced in. The 50's opened up and the 30 on the starboard side. Sammy was working his M16. The Lieutenant was hunkered down on the deck, his rifle curled up to his chest like it was his long-lost kid. What a waste. I can't even imagine someone following him into battle. JJ looked over and grinned and rolled his eyes. Pathetic.

I hit the pier a little harder than I intended but Sammy was on the ball and jumped onto the pier and stopped the boat from slamming into it too hard. The front 50's and starboard 30 were still in action. Frank jumped out on the pier and I started handing ammo off. They started stacking it and I continued to feed them.

"Get over here and help me," I yelled to the Lieutenant but he just laid on the deck, whimpering.

I considered either shooting him or throwing him over the side but decided to just go about offloading. Three men came running down and started grabbing the ammo.

"Man, that was cutting it close. We are down to our last few rounds," one of them said before taking off running loaded down with the crates of munitions.

The other boats were standing offshore pounding the VC as well. When we were finished, my guys jumped in and I pulled out so the second boat could dock. We rotated until we were all off loaded and the VC had finally broken off the attack.

CHAPTER THIRTY-EIGHT

We moored at the pier and went up to the base. You could see that they had been hit very hard. Little was standing. The soldiers and sailors were gathering the dead and wounded. The commanding officer was among one of the injured. A medic was working on his leg.

"I can't thank you boys enough. Without your firepower, they would have overrun us for sure. Those 50's helped swing the battle."

"Glad we got here in time. We ran flat out the entire way. How about we hang around and help out wherever we are needed?" I offered.

"We sure could use the help. Thank you for the offer. How many men can you spare?" he asked.

"We can all stay a couple days if that would help. I'll need to get an okay from Captain Willard," I replied.

"JT Willard?"

"Captain James Willard, yes sir."

"Excellent. I'll make the call. We went to the academy together," he replied smiling.

While he was taking care of that, I went and told the crew what was happening. Pretty much everyone was eager to help. A couple groaned but that's almost always the case. The Lieutenant was waiting to talk to me. As soon as I sent the men off he grabbed my arm.

"I want to be sent back to Ben Keo immediately."

"You'll have to talk to the base Commander about that," I replied.

"I thought you were in charge. That's what you said. What happened?" he challenged.

"I said on the boat I was the Captain and was in total charge. We are now going to be on the base. Just like at Ben Keo or anyplace else, I relinquish the command to the senior officer."

"So, you refuse to send me back?"

"Lieutenant, it's not my call. Go talk to the Commander."

"What about the After-Action-Report?"

"What about it?"

"I want to know what you are going to put in it," he insisted.

"Exactly what happened. What our part was during the enemy contact," I replied.

"Do you intend to mention anything about me?"

I looked at him for several moments. I could just let the whole thing go but that would not only be dishonest but worse, a disservice to those that may have to serve under him some day. He was a coward in my book.

I said, "Like all After-Action Reports, it will describe what we did as a team. If anyone went above and beyond and deserves special recognition, it will be noted. It will point out how each individual contributed to the success of the mission."

"I'm asking what you intend to say about me," he said, taking a step closer.

He was in my personal space and I'm not real big on people crowding me. Rather than step back, I decided to hold my ground and just stare him down.

"Lieutenant, I will submit my report to Lieutenant Keeler upon return to base. He will in turn hand it over to Captain Willard. You know how it works. It gets sent up the line to people above my pay grade," I replied.

"I want to see it first," he demanded.

"Sorry, you're not in my chain of command. It goes to Lieutenant Keeler first. You want to see it? Talk to him. Now excuse me, I have work to do. You are welcome to pitch in and help out," I said and walked away before he could say another word.

I wondered what kind of stink this was going to make but what was the worse they could do? Send me to Vietnam? We spent the next three days digging trenches, filling sandbags, helping make the CP more secure, and any other task we could help with. I never once saw the Lieutenant getting his hands dirty. People like him have no place in the Navy or any other branch of the military.

The base Commander came down to the boat to see us off and offer his thanks. I noticed he kept looking at Lieutenant Bollard.

"Is he with you?" he asked.

I replied in a low voice, "No sir, not really. He wouldn't fight and he didn't lift a finger to help here."

Lord, I was taking a huge chance in saying that to the Commander. He looked at me for a second, I could almost hear the gears turning over in his head. He rubbed his chin with his hand for a second.

"Make sure that gets in the After-Action-Report. You can say that I will attest to the fact that he did nothing to help here."

"Aye, Aye, sir. Thank you," I replied.

"I'll call JT and fill him in as well. We don't need officers like that in this man's Navy," he said.

"I agree totally."

***

When we got back the LT was at the pier waiting for us.

"The Captain would like to have a word with you," he said.

"Yes sir."

He walked with me back to the CP and said, "You can go on in. He is anxious to talk to you.

I took a deep breath entered his office.

"Ah, First-Class French. At ease. Please, have a seat and tell me about what happened at Nan Ke Lo. Both on the way and once you got there," he said leaning back in his chair.

Here I was, at the moment of truth. I hadn't even finished the After-

Action-Report and it was beginning. I took a deep breath and began.

"We raced full speed to Nan Ke Lo. We knew it was a critical mission. When we got there, the base was..."

"Hold it. Tell me about Lieutenant Bollard. I want the specifics, and don't leave anything out," he cautioned.

"Sir, I am very uncomfortable with this. Mr. Bollard is an officer and I'm just an enlisted man. I'm not sure I should tell everything that happened."

"First Class French, I want to know what happened," the Captain said.

"The Lieutenant tried on several occasions to counterman my orders. Things like not going into the pier to off load. He wanted to dump it someplace else and let them get it. He told me he was an officer and I was just an enlisted man and he didn't take orders from me. He raised his M16 at me and said it was an order. My men dissuaded him from shooting me. During the run to the pier, he dropped down on the deck and hugged his gun to his chest and refused to fire his weapon. I mean, it wasn't even that bad on the boat. We had the 50's from all four boats pounding the shore and VC. They took off pretty quickly after we let loose. Then, when the VC broke off, I went to talk to the base Commander and, well, as you know, he called to see if we could stay and help put the camp back together."

"And what was Bollard's part in helping at the base."

"Sir, all I can say is that I never saw him except at chow on a couple of occasions. I talked to the boat crews and they never saw him either."

"Are you willing to go on record with these statements?" the Captain asked.

"I am sir."

"Alright. I would like for you to bring your After-Action-Report directly to me. No one is to see it but me, understood."

"Aye, aye, sir."

"I know you are tired but, I would like it on my desk by 0:800 tomorrow."

"Aye, aye, sir."

I wasn't sure what to make of the meeting. Was he going to just bury it so the Lieutenant would just skate? I'm not foolish enough to believe enlisted are treated the same as officers. It's like the laws for the rich and the poor. The only motivation I had was to think about what would it be like for the men under his command. What if he got to a combat position? He was not a leader and he could get a lot of good men killed. The only thing I could say is that I was ordered to tell what had transpired. I don't feel I exaggerated and whatever happened was of the Lieutenant's own doing.

CHAPTER THIRTY-NINE

I sealed the report and wrote **FOR THE CAPTAIN'S EYES ONLY**. I had it on his desk before he arrived for the morning. As I was eating, the LT came over and sat down next to me.

"Well, a hornet's nest has sure been shaken."

"Yeah, I kind of figured that," I replied.

"Bollard wants to have you Court Martialed for insubordination and refusing a direct order."

I just shrugged. What was I going to say? It wasn't exactly unexpected. He was following up on his threat.

"There it is," I said, finishing my eggs and turning in my tray.

"Don't worry, we have your back," he said as he walked off.

I heard nothing further the rest of the day and our patrol that night was about as routine as they get with only a couple of tense moments but nothing serious. From the sounds on the river, it must have been quiet all around us. I heard a few outgoing artillery rounds but they were probably more for harassment than an actual fire support mission.

It was so quiet it made me slightly paranoid. I wondered if ol' Charlie was planning another Tet type operation. It's strange, when things get too quiet you start to get suspicious of what the enemy is up to.

When we got back, we debriefed with the next boats going out and headed to eat and then to our racks. I was so tired I almost blew off lunch but as it turned out they were having a hamburger and hot dog cook out. After I had wolfed down two hamburgers and a hot dog, I headed to the hooch to get some sleep. No one was there and it was easy to see why. It must have been a hundred plus inside. I headed down to the boat and found everyone sprawled out. I found a place and crashed along with the rest of them.

It was two days later when I was called to the Captain's office. I had been apprehensive, wondering when the SHTF. I was glad to finally address the situation.

"Martin French, reporting as ordered, sir," said, standing at attention.

"At ease French. Grab a seat."

I sat down in the one directly across from his desk.

"I have had time to investigate the incident concerning Lieutenant Bollard. As you know, the Lieutenant wanted you brought up on charges of insubordination and failing to respond to a direct order."

"Yes, sir."

"In my investigation, I found you acted within the scope of your authority as the boat captain. Lieutenant Bollard did not recognize your authority and that is his error. He also threatened you by raising his weapon. I find him guilty of dereliction of duty and of cowardness. He failed to project the proper image as a leader and an officer. I have recommended that the Lieutenant be Court Martialed. He will be flown to Saigon where the trial will be held. At this point, I am not sure if you will be called to testify against Lieutenant Bollard. I will be informed of the court's decision on that matter."

I let out a sigh and said, "Thank you sir."

"Captain French, you acted exactly as you should have. Your actions and the other boats helped beat off the VC attacked and saved American lives. The Navy does not need men like Lieutenant Bollard. I know we are at war, but we are better off without his kind of leadership. You are formally notified that no action against you or your crew will be forthcoming. You are dismissed Captain French," he said standing and walked around with his hand extended.

He said, "Son, if we had a few hundred more like you, this war would be a lot shorter."

"Thank you, sir," I said.

Walking back to the boat I felt a hundred pounds lighter. I knew I was in the right but there is always this nagging doubt in the back of your head. You ask yourself if you handled it the best way possible? Did you cross the line at some point? And even if you are sure, the doubt remains until you hear that it is over officially. I was hoping I wouldn't have to go to Saigon to testify against the Lieutenant. I had no desire to rub salt in his wounds. His career was over and I didn't want to make it seem like I was gloating.

***

As it turned out, it was filtered through the grapevine that the Lieutenant decided to resign his commission rather than face a General

Court Martial. He lost all military benefits as part of the deal. All I cared about was that it was the end of it for me.

The next three months were mostly routine. Boredom for part of the day followed by full tilt adrenalin rush during firefights. Some days we would go the entire patrol and nothing would happen that was noteworthy. Other days it seemed like from the time we left base until our patrol was over, we were on pins and needles.

One thing that became noticeable was the behavior of members of the crew when it came time for them to rotate back to the world. Frank Bauer started carrying a thumper and the minute a shot came toward our patrol he would unload six or seven rounds. When he finally left, he was a nervous wreck. In some ways, I was ready for him to leave. He was spooking all of us. His replacement was an NFG named Tony "Space Cadet" Spacer, who didn't belong in Vietnam, but in all honesty, who did?

Sammy was the next to leave. He counted down the time in hours instead of days. I got tired of hearing the update every few hours. Like

Bauer, I was more than ready to say goodbye to him when he finally left.

When it came my turn, I didn't want to be like them. It would demoralize the crew and I couldn't have that. Sammy was replaced by James "Mickey" Cotton. He was called 'Mickey' because of his big ears that stuck out from the side of his head. He also had a high-pitched voice that seemed to go with the character he was named after. He had been in country for six months and had come from another base as a replacement.

What bothered me the most was how easy it was to kill. If it moved, we unloaded on it. Anytime a shot came from a village we would literally blow it to hell. On a couple of occasions, we went ashore and burned the village to the ground. Killing became a way of life. You didn't even have to think about it. I was starting to worry about my mental state. What the hell was I going to be like once I became a civilian again?

I brooded about this for several weeks as my days began to count down. I found I started doing like everyone else. Keeping a mental calendar running in my head.

I was finally getting 'short' but I had a crew that depended on me and I couldn't let my guard down. If possible, I became even more vigilant. I was sure we would be attacked around every bend or narrow tributary that we explored.

CHAPTER FORTY

Ten and a wake up to go, the SHTF. During what seemed like a routine stop on a sampan, all hell broke loose. Spacer had boarded the sampan to check out the cargo. He was looking through the sacks of rice when he disappeared into the back further.

I just happened to look where he had gone when I saw the nose of an RPG poke out.

"RPG," I screamed and slammed the throttles forward hoping to dislodge the shooter.

WOOSH, the sound of the rocket being fired filled my ears. It hit the port corner of the boat and exploded. We were thrown around and I landed on the deck. AK fire erupted and we all opened up on the sampan.

I felt a burning sensation in my side and was knocked to the deck a second time. I staggered to my feet and slammed the throttles forward, dragging the sampan along with us. Everyone else was firing into the boat.

I reached over and cut the sampan loose and we circled back around to come up behind it. Iggy was on the 50's, ready to riddle the damn thing.

There was no sound except for the water lapping on the side of the boat.

"Hey Space Cadet, are you in there?"

Nothing.

"Spacer are you alive?" I yelled.

I nodded to Mickey and JJ to secure the boat to the sampan. I had them go aboard and check it out. Everyone on board was dead. They found Tony Spacer with his throat slit. At least we hadn't been the ones that killed him.

The boat held boxes of mortar rounds and several cases of RPG. Why they were trying to slip it by us in broad day light was a mystery to me.

They brought Tony's body on board, cut the sampan loose and we blew the hell out of it until it sank. They wouldn't be getting their hands on these weapons.

My side was burning and I looked down and saw where the bullet had entered. I felt around and found the exit wound. At least it had gone right through me.

"Geez captain. You're bleeding like a stuck pig. You need to sit down. I'll handle the boat," JJ said and helped me to the floor.

Iggy came over and wrapped a battle dressing around me and pulled it tight.

"Morphine?" he asked.

"No. I'm fine. Just a little discomfort. Have JJ call in a sit-rep and let them know what happened and that we are headed back," I said.

"On it skipper," JJ said from the wheelhouse.

I must have blacked out because the next thing I remember is being lifted into a Medavac.

"You're going to be okay Iceman. I wanted to say goodbye in case I don't see you again," Lieutenant Keeler said.

"Thanks LT. Been great serving with you."

With that I was loaded on the chopper and the next thing I knew I was in the cool air of the higher altitudes gliding over Vietnam.

I was flown to the hospital ship, the USS Sanctuary. I remember very little about it. I went into surgery, was operated on, and the next thing I remember was waking up in recovery like the last time.

While lying in bed I realized I had seven and a wake up and I would be going back to the US. I wasn't sure how I felt about that. On one hand, I was ready to leave this stinking dung hole but a small part of me would miss the adventure.

While I was on the ship I received my second purple heart. This one I felt I had earned. I got a physical, my teeth checked out, and poked and prodded and was pronounced fit to join humanity once again.

***

POSTSCRIPT

Vietnam was at war long before the US intervened. They had been at war since the mid-1940's when Japan tried to seize the country. Many countries have tried and failed at bringing Vietnam under control.

Under Ho-Chi-Min, no nation has been able to conquer Vietnam regardless of their technology or superior firepower. Ho-Chi-Min and his ragtag armies have been able to defend the country no matter what nation tries to invade them.

Before the war was over, 2,594,000 would serve in Vietnam. 303,644 American military men and women would be treated for wounds during the war. An astounding 97.4 percent of those treated survived.

58,220 American soldiers died during that period. Some people call it a 'Conflict'; they were obviously not in the military during that time.

Not all that served in Vietnam have returned home or been accounted for. We still have POW's and MIA's. The war was not lost by the American Soldiers but by a President and the Advisors that were arrogant, egotistical, and ignorant of what it took to win the war.

During the time frame of 1965 – 1974 when the US relieved the French trapped in the Vietnam war, there was an estimated 4 million civilian casualties. 86.5 % of the American casualties were white; 12.5 % were black; 1.0 were all other races combined.

President Johnson and his so-called advisors, tried to micromanage the war from Washington D.C. Instead of letting the soldiers on the ground and frontlines take control, people like Robert McNamara, the "Wise-Men", and to some extent, Westmoreland, who was LBJ's puppet General, thought they could win with 'body count'.

They never had a plan for actually winning the war, so they sacrificed American lives for a no clear-cut objective. It was a waste of lives of the Army, Navy, Coast Guard, Air Force, and Marine soldiers and sailors that were not even accepted when they returned home.

Korean and Vietnam veterans are the most underappreciated men and women to have ever served the American people.

ABOUT THE AUTHOR

Marshall W. Huffman began writing after he retired from teaching. He decided to start with a trilogy based on a cataclysmic event. Marshall's first trilogy is *THE EVENT* and consists of Book I - *THE END*, Book-ii - *THE BEGINNING*, and Book III - *THE REVELATION*. With *THE EVENTS* success, he decided to write a second trilogy that is a frightening look at the events that could lead to *THE SECOND CIVIL WAR*. It is made up of: Book I – A NATION DIVIDED; BOOK II – A NATION AT WAR; BOOK III – A NATION HEALING.

Marshall was born in Bainbridge, Georgia and grew up in Indiana. After spending eight years in the Navy (1964-1972), he attended Ball State University, earning a B.S. degree in Business.

During and after college, he was involved in the restaurant business and spent the next twenty-five years in all types of venues, eventually owing his own fine dining restaurant. After years of long hours, he decided on a career change. He attended Eastern Illinois University earning an MBA. Because of his business background, Eastern Illinois University asked him to teach in the hospitality management program while enrolled in the University of Illinois PhD program.

He was recruited from Eastern to Parkland College and soon took over as the Program Director for the Hospitality Program. During his tenure there, he became a chef and had a television show called *Cooking around the World with Chef Marshall* and taught a series of Gourmet cooking classes for Continuing Education as well.

Professor Huffman retired from teaching along with his wife, Dr. Susan Huffman, to the Tampa Bay Florida area. He has published over 50 Novels.

You can find his books under:

MARSHALL HUFFMAN at

Amazon.com. and at
mwhuffman.com